TURBULENCE

TURBULENCE

JAN MARK

Hodder
Children's
Books

A division of Hodder Headline Limited

A Catalogue record for this book is available from
the British Library

ISBN 0 340 86099 5

Typeset in Palatino by Avon DataSet Ltd,
Bidford-on-Avon, Warwickshire

Printed and bound in Great Britain by
Bookmarque Ltd, Croydon, Surrey

The paper and board used in this paperback by
Hodder Children's Books are natural recyclable products
made from wood grown in sustainable forests.
The manufacturing processes conform to the environmental
regulations of the country of origin.

Hodder Children's Books
a division of Hodder Headline Ltd
338 Euston Road
London NW1 3BH

For Anne McNeil

One

No one much liked the idea of my paper round but no one argued – much. When you can look one parent in the eye and the other in the eyebrow, arguments are carried out on a more equal footing than when you are down at shoulder lever whining, 'It's not fair.'

'Might as well go out with a banner: "Abduct Me",' Gran said. Even Mr Mirza at the newsagent's was a bit doubtful when I went in about his advert. He is very protective, but the Mirzas had only just taken over the shop and were anxious to hang on to their customers. Mr Mirza barely comes up to my ear. I soon convinced him.

Mum said, 'What about the dark winter mornings?'

I love the dark winter mornings. They remind me how far north this country is. In Canada, at our latitude, they practically have polar bears raiding the dustbins. I love the fact that even with British Summer

Time you can't hold back the darkness indefinitely, any more than you can stop the tides. I love the stillness, even so near the centre of town, although that doesn't last long. It's amazing how many people are already about when the shop opens at six am, milkmen, postmen, joggers – especially the lumpy ones who don't want to be seen in daylight, the early buses all brightly lit and roaring down the main road, picking up people going to work, heading for the station. However cold and wet and tired and fed up you are it must be a cheering moment when that first bus comes into sight.

By the time I get back to the shop the binmen are on the road, followed by the recycling truck, all clangour and flashing lights, and the paper boys – who are younger and punier than me – are just arriving to collect their bags. We're a class of society on our own, an elite, I like to think, people who operate on a different timescale from the rest of the population; not just morning people, dawn people. (Sandor was a morning person except when he was being an evening person. It depended upon who he was talking to.) We see the world from another perspective, almost another plane. We are the ones making things happen, getting things going, not movers and shakers, *deliverers*. We are the day's midwives, I thought once, coasting down Addington Road; the first line of a poem. Fortunately it never went any further. I had been thinking of a real poem, by John Donne: ' 'Tis the year's midnight, and it is the day's,' because it happened to be the morning of the year's midnight, the shortest day, although the mornings don't start getting lighter till after the New Year. You notice that kind of thing when you're out before sunrise.

The best thing about the paper round though, apart from the money, was that I could be certain of being out of the house while everyone else was getting up.

I chained my bike to our railings which somehow escaped being melted down to make tanks during World War II and have spearheads on them. The house is old enough to have what estate agents describe as 'original features', such as draughts. Our original feature is the railings. As I went in Mum called out, 'Is that you, Clay?'

Who else would it be, crashing in just as everyone else was crawling out? 'Yes, it's me, Clay.' Clare, actually, but when I was little I pronounced it Clay,

3

and it stuck, which was fine because unlike most baby names it is much tougher than the real one. Clay Winchester (after whom they named the repeating rifle that won the West, the Winchester 73) rides into town, out of the desert, hitches Ol' Betsey to the rail outside the saloon on Main Street and moseys on down to the OK Corral for a shoot-out with the Clantons. Eat your heart out, Wyatt Earp, Clay Winchester was there first, blowing the smoke from her pearl-handled Colts by the time you and your brothers and Doc Holliday got your sorry asses into gear. Clay rides shotgun on the Deadwood Stage. That Winchester dame can knock the pip out of an ace at one hundred paces and never plays poker with her back to an open door. Out here in the badlands we all know what happened to James Butler Hickok, Wild Bill to his friends and foes. I knew him well.

Etcetera. Somewhere in the upper branches of the family tree sits a gorilla, that's my theory. Most of the relatives are clearly descended from lemurs and marmosets, but now and again one of us turns out heavy and big-boned and powerful. In this generation, I got the gorilla gene.

Mum – one of the marmosets – was in the kitchen. The days when we could look each other in the eye were long gone. Now she was scurrying round my ankles.

'Couldn't you have brought the milk in?'

The milkman hadn't arrived when I went out, we're on the end of his route. See, I know about things like that. 'There's none on the step.'

'Someone's nicked it again.' She sighed and wrote 'milk' on the board by the door. We do go through the motions of being organized. 'Can you get some on the way home in case I forget?'

This is not a rough neighbourhood but some of the houses are occupied by students and other opportunists. Our milk thief was a regular like the window cleaner, and, to give him his due, he seemed to share his thieving out fairly. We only lost ours about once a month.

'Is there enough for cornflakes?' I looked in the fridge. There wasn't. 'I'll borrow some of Dad's.'

'If you want to drink cottage cheese. It's probably been there for days. I'll put some toast on.'

'I'll do it, you go and get ready. I'll see if Dad needs anything else and shop on my way home.'

'Yes, *you* won't forget,' Mum said. Marmosets have big wistful eyes. Reliable Clay the Gorilla nodded reassuringly and shooed her out. I heard her going upstairs and then there was a scrum on the landing as someone, probably a grandmother, tried to get into the bathroom at the same moment. I put the toast on hold and went down the garden to the studio where Dad, the other morning Winchester, would already be getting stuck in to a day's work.

He wasn't, in fact, doing anything of the sort, but like me he got the hell out before anyone else started blundering around, moving at lightning speed: loo, shower, shave, down to the studio before the mist had cleared from the bathroom mirror.

We never called it a shed; Sandor did. When Gran moved in with us Dad invested in a big, sturdy wooden outbuilding, properly wired for computer, lights and heat, and cleared out the room he used as a studio to make room for Gran. We called the new building the studio because that's what it was. Even though it was at the end of the garden by the vegetables, we didn't think of it as a shed. Dad has a microwave and a little fridge in there, and coffee things, so that he doesn't have to break off work and come up to the house when he needs refuelling, but he never remembers to put the milk away at night, hence Mum's crack about the cottage cheese.

It is on a proper hard standing – he'd had to get planning permission for it – with steps up to the door. When I went in he was standing with his coffee mug, staring up the garden through the window over his desk. It was the best view of the garden then – you couldn't see the studio, although the Russian vine has covered it now.

'Do you want anything in town?' I said. 'And go easy on the milk. Dairy Man has been at work again.'

'He must watch our every move,' Dad said. 'He must know what time you go out and then sneak from his lair and make a dash for the doorstep as soon as the milkman's been. If we put our minds to it we could probably catch the bugger.'

'He won't be round again till Easter,' I said, 'if my suspicions are correct.'

'He's affected by the full moon?'

'No, he just steals from different doorsteps each time. I checked with the Gardiners at 37. They lose theirs four days after we do but Mrs G says he never takes the cranberry juice. He must have an allergy – and don't say anything to Mum about him watching my movements. She'll start worrying it's me he's after.'

'Good point; the optimistic fool.' The Mac started yattering to itself. Dad turned to it.

'Do you need anything?'

'No – hey, don't we have company this evening? Aren't I supposed to be going to Sainsbury's?'

'It's Thursday. Mum's got people coming tomorrow.' Dad too has a board by the door. I wrote, 'Friday – TOMORROW! – Sainsbury's.' Necessary for a man who does not know what day of the week it is. Later I would erase 'MORROW' and substitute 'DAY'. 'See you tonight.'

He was bending over the keyboard already.

'Have a good day – watch out for the Canadians.'

The house is a VHS-free zone; DVD rules. When the state-of-the-art integrated digital system was installed the old video recorder went down to the shed – studio – with the old telly. In the back room we watch shiny new movies on the shiny new flat screen. In the studio Dad and I have our collection of Westerns, mostly black and white, and minority movies. We call them that because they are watched by a minority, me and Dad. Half the time no one else has ever heard of them, much less seen them. We have an acid test for new friends – or rather, new acquaintances; they only become true friends if they pass it. We ask if they've seen something we really like, and if they have, they're half-way in. If they're prepared to give it a try that's a good sign. If they enjoy it, they're one of us.

Or rather, we pretend that this is what we'd do. 'Think he's up for *Ulysses' Gaze*?' Dad mutters (we haven't yet met anyone else who's seen it) or I'll give the once-over to some woman Gran's brought home. 'How about *Nosferatu*, the original, not the remake?'

Dad likes to create improbable double-bills on one cassette: *The Wizard of Oz* and *Aguirre, Wrath of God* or, my favourite, *The Railway Children* and *McCabe and Mrs Miller* which is about two people running a brothel.

One on its own, because we haven't found anything worthy to pair with it, is a Canadian film called *Careful* which Dad taped off Channel 4, years ago. It is about people living in fear of an avalanche and is seriously weird, being set on a mountain and apparently shot in somebody's house, possibly under the stairs.

'All Canadian movies are weird,' Dad said. 'Look at David Cronenberg. It's part of the plot.'

'What plot?'

'People think Canadians are boring mainly, as far as I can see, because singly and collectively they kill very few of each other or anyone else. This is a ruse. Because they seem dull no one notices what they are really doing, which is planning to take over the world. Who shot JFK?'

'Who did?'

'Obvious, isn't it?'

After that, when anyone came up with a really crazy conspiracy theory, we knew the truth. President Kennedy, Marilyn Monroe, the Twin Towers, Princess Diana ... Dad and I would look at each other significantly.

'Canadians.'

The last job of the morning before school was making sure that everyone was out of the house. In summer this was a simple matter of counting bicycles but it was cold that day and looked like rain. There were still two bikes as well as mine, chained to the railings; Rosie's and Jamie's. They might have decided to get the bus to school, being weedy marmosets, but it was quite likely that Rosie was still buffing her nails and selecting lip gloss for the Barbie lookalike contest which was Year Six at Grosvenor Road. If Jamie wasn't off the premises he might have gone to sleep again. When I looked round his door the curtains were still drawn but the duvet was on the floor and he wasn't under it. I kicked it to make sure, and opened the transom to get a bit of oxygen into the room, a strange colourless gas, unknown to Jamie.

Rosie passed me as I came out, heading for the stairs, and looking over the landing banister I saw Jamie ambling along the hall like one of those dozy bumblebees that have OD'd on pollen and can't get airborne. They were both going to be late whether they cycled or caught a bus, but that wasn't my problem. Teachers at school were very good about not asking me why James – which he had taken to spelling Jamze in the interests of cool – was such a waste of precious resources, let alone space. Think how much he was contributing to the depletion of the ozone layer just by farting.

'It's his age,' Mum said helplessly, muttering about hormones.

'Were you like that at fourteen?' I asked Dad once.

'I was at work at his age,' Dad said. 'We didn't have hormones, we had the print unions.'

We know two kinds of people, the ones we make an effort for and the ones who'd be surprised if we did. The second sort are the friends who go back years with

Mum and Dad, who turn up carrying bottles, and at some point in the evening one of us remembers to put the oven on and food appears. Last one standing locks up. I've usually bailed out by eleven on account of the paper round. Jamze probably will not show up at all and Rosie will stick around long enough to be noticed before zipping upstairs again to get on with texting friends she can practically see from the bedroom window. Rosie's method of getting noticed is to start a row with somebody older and bigger (all of us) so she can retire in tears leaving us looking like big heartless bullies. We are supposed to feel guilty but this doesn't happen very often.

When we are making an effort most of the effort goes into ensuring that neither of them puts in an appearance and then working out which of the ones who are left actually want to be there. It's a tight squeeze with more than six around the table for a sit-down meal, so anyone who would really, truly prefer to be somewhere else is never pressured into staying.

Gran only ever asks one question: 'Do they play bridge?' If the answer is yes she is off like a shot having once gone on holiday on the Isle of Wight and been trapped for a week among bridge players who converted Grandad and turned him into a bridge bore overnight.

'The marriage survived but he was never the same again,' she tells people mournfully.

Gran does not know about our Canadian theory, she has one of her own. 'Bridge players are a species of vampire. Once bitten by a vampire you become one too. Bridge players will not rest until the whole world has been bitten. They are the undead. And look at *The Invasion of the Body Snatchers*. Everyone thinks that was a metaphor for the Red Menace, commie infiltration. No it wasn't. It was a subconscious fear of bridge players.'

The ones coming on Friday night were the Iversons, whom we'd known for ever, and some people Mum had met at work who were new to the area. She wanted to make them feel welcome, help them make friends:

Gran: Bridge players?

Mum: I don't know.

Gran: Then they aren't. If they were you'd know all about it, every hand they'd ever played. Opening bids going back to 1960.

Mum: I don't think he does. She might.

Gran: It'll be both or neither. Otherwise one would have murdered the other by now. I'll give it a whirl.

Mum: (Mentally counting place settings and calculating elbow room – literally) You don't have to.

Gran: If you want me to go out, why not say so? I can walk the streets till midnight. I don't suppose anyone will molest me but you can imagine the headlines, can't you? 'Widow ejected from dinner party. Left to die.' The local rag will have a field day: 'Frail grandmother, Marina Morton, 63, was found huddled in a windswept doorway in the early hours of Saturday morning. Friends told the *Courier*, "Marina always dreaded being a burden to her family. She lived on twigs . . ." '

Mum: If you're going to give anything a whirl, why not a noose? Tie it to the attic banisters – it's a good six-metre drop.

Gran: I'm leaving everything to the rehab centre, you know that. And there's a codicil in my will: 'If I'm found dead in suspicious circumstances, arrest my daughter.'

I left them to it and went to lay the table. It was six thirty – pm – and everyone had finally woken up. Sometimes, in the mornings, not a word is exchanged while they all stagger around blearily and only notice each other if someone forgets to lock the bathroom door. This is what I miss by leaving for Mirzas' before anyone else is up. There would be eight for dinner, Mum, Dad, me, Gran – who far from frail is another gorilla – John and Penny Iverson and the New Couple. I hadn't got around to asking who they were yet, but I hoped they were thin.

The room looked nice. The folding glass doors between front and back had been opened, the fire was lit, the curtains drawn. Gran had vacuumed as soon as she got home and all the debris had been cleared away. There is a seat that lifts up in the front bay window. It's understood that if we've got people coming round who it's worth tidying up for, anything that isn't removed before Gran gets the hoover out goes into the window seat. When the seat won't close, we have a clear out.

Dad had done the Sainsbury's run and remembered to bring home cut flowers. All that needed doing now was to get Jamze and Rosie sorted before seven o'clock, then we could all take turns at a lightning shower or bath so as to be clean and ready when the guests arrived, sitting around beaming, the perfect family. We wouldn't have bothered to do perfect for John and Penny, this was all in aid of Mr and Mrs New. I thought I'd better nip down the garden and weed Dad out of the studio so that he'd be on the starting blocks when it was his turn for the bathroom.

He was closing down for the night when I went in.

'Who are these people?' he said; not that he minded who they were, it just hadn't occurred to him to ask before.

'He started work at DDI last month. She's his partner, I suppose; wife.'

'Names?'

'Dunno. Mum may remember to tell us before they get here.'

'Hasn't she told you?'

'She might have done. It didn't stick.'

It wasn't that we didn't care, but in a house where everyone was always rushing off in different directions it was often difficult to remember who had been told what. Gran had promised, 'When I retire I'll stay at home all day and become the tranquil heart of the household. I shall sit by the window in what will be known as Grandmother's Chair – when it stands

16

reproachfully empty for the last time – and you will all come to me with your little joys and sorrows.'

'When you retire,' Mum said, 'you'll take to absinthe and spend all day watching *I Married a Slime Mould* and *Zombie Dawn* and I'll have to clear up your roaches.'

Dad and I do not entirely share Gran's taste in cinema but her collection, like ours, has been mainly taped off late-night television so it has to be watched in the studio. She wanders in with a video, when she knows Dad is finishing work:

Gran: You don't mind do you, Roj?

Dad: Feel free. Would I be interested?

Gran: I don't think so, it's *Night of the Living Dead* and *The Wolf Man*.

Dad: (Scanning our library) We've got *Night of the Living Dead*.

Gran: Yes, but yours is paired with *Dumbo*. I don't want to be moved to tears. At the end of a long day I crave blood and guts.

Dad: Would you like me to get you *The Texas Chainsaw Massacre* for Christmas?

Gran: Kid's stuff. No thank you, I like my viscera unravelled with a bit of finesse.

17

The Iversons arrived first. When I went to let them in I could hear them arguing on the doorstep about whose turn it was to drive home. They were always arguing. I'd have known it was them outside even if I hadn't expected it to be, but it never seemed to get as far as an outright row. Like us, really. We're always arguing but it's just the way we talk to each other. They'd been together as long as Mum and Dad.

'Remind me,' John Iverson said as they came in, 'who are the others? Are they here yet?'

'Mr and Mrs Parker, I think. Or Harker. No, they're not.'

Dad looked out of the front room door.

'Who's driving?'

'I am,' Penny said. 'I don't believe it's my turn but anything for a quiet life.'

'You forget,' John said, 'I drove home from the Abbasis' do.'

'That doesn't count, they're Muslims. No one was drinking.'

'You know,' Dad said, mildly, 'you could always get a cab. You're not exactly short of a bob or two.'

I thought, while I was hanging up coats, that if people at school talked to each other like that there would be massive strops or a punch up, if it was certain people, and sulks and mutterings in corners, and friends you always walked home with would start walking with someone else. Penny just laughed and said, 'All right for you, Roger; house full of wage earners. How's the paper round, Clay?'

I wouldn't call my earnings a wage, exactly, but it was nice to be included in the economy.

We all went into the living room, the front end, and sat around the fire. Mum was in the kitchen looking after the food so Gran served drinks and I started the nibbles circulating. Then the doorbell rang again.

'I'm nearest!' Mum, who was just coming in to say hullo, backed out again. There were voices, greetings, and then they were in the room, Mr and Mrs New. I don't remember them walking through the doorway, it was more as if they had descended among us or rather, he had and she'd come down with him.

At first I thought they were in evening dress. I was putting on a CD, something bland and backgroundy, so my first sight was a tail-of-the-eye impression and the impression was gloss. They gleamed, and everything else in the room, from the furniture to the family, lost several degrees of definition. The colour faded in the curtains, the wattage dropped. Gran and Dad turned grey. I was kneeling on the floor so I probably merged with the carpet, like a chameleon.

Then Mum started making introductions and people spoke and the contrast went back to normal.

'This is Ali and Sandor Harker – Roger, my husband; Marina, my mother; John and Penny Iverson.' Everyone was saying hullo and good evening and Mr Harker, Sandor, was shaking hands. People don't usually shake hands with us. I got the additional impression that he was bowing slightly; perhaps he was foreign, his name sounded foreign. Ali just said 'Hi,' and smiled and in between smiles she looked adoringly at Sandor. One thing you learn from watching movies: once you've made an establishing shot, you should leave well alone. There is a limit to how long people want to look at one facial expression. I was thinking, You're married, aren't you? You've got him. You must be used to him by now – or can't you believe your luck? He was very good-looking, they both were, that was why the room had seemed to fade out, they absorbed all the light and energy. I wasn't sure that he felt quite so lucky as she did but he knew how lucky she was – no, I didn't think that then. It came to me much later.

'Where's Clay?' Mum said. I am usually hard to miss, like Gran, and I wished that I hadn't been kneeling when the Harkers came in because now I was going to have to stand up. That can seriously interfere with a room's proportions.

Instead, Sandor Harker noticed that I was the only one who hadn't been introduced, came over, stooped in courtly fashion as seen in Gainsborough Studio films of the 1940s, and took my hand. For a second I could have sworn he was going to kiss it, but at the same time I noticed that he was a big guy so I stood up anyway and gave his hand a hearty shake in a down-home-folks sort of way. Welcome to the spread, ol' buddy.

He could have carried Ali around on his shoulder like an organ-grinder's monkey – not that there was anything simian about her, but in the ancestor department I reckoned bush babies. No anthropoid apes up that family tree. At least she wouldn't take up much room at dinner.

When it was time to sit down I manoeuvred Ali between Gran and John Iverson who is almost as wide as he is high. Mum sat at one end and I was next to her so that we could get in and out easily with plates and food. I didn't take much notice of where Sandor was sitting until he started talking.

He'd been talking all the time, I suppose, through the first course, which was soup, and I'd slurped mine down so as to get back to the kitchen to keep an eye on the steamer. It was when I was carrying in the vegetables that I took in that he was sitting at the far end, where Dad ought to have been, head of the household and all that, if we ever bothered about such things. Perhaps we should have bothered. Dad was next to me with Penny on his other side. It was a bit odd, as if he was sitting there in the middle because there was nowhere else. And every head was turned in Sandor's direction. He wasn't holding forth and he didn't seem to be saying anything very amazing, it was just that the others weren't talking to each other, they were listening to him. What he was doing was asking them what they did, almost as if he was interviewing them, but sounding absolutely bowled over by the news that Penny ran a craft shop and John was in publishing and Gran was a deputy head teacher and Dad a graphic designer. I assumed he knew what Mum did since they were both at DDI. He was the perfect host, putting everyone at their ease and making them feel at home, only he wasn't the host and it wasn't his home.

People took their cues from him. No one said anything about the food until he praised it and then everyone praised it and all the heads swivelled away from him and pointed towards Mum as if he had reversed the polarity. Mum just seemed pleased that the party was going well. I wondered what Dad thought. At the end of the main course he leaned across to Ali Harker and said, 'And what do you do?'

Ali peeled her gaze away from Sandor and said vaguely, 'I've got a job . . .'

She might have gone on to tell us what it was but Sandor butted in.

'She works for Kentigern.'

'Oh, you're in publishing too,' John Iverson said. Ali blushed and laughed as if Sandor had let on that she earned her living lap-dancing, and didn't say anything else because Sandor was now talking to John Iverson about Kentigern Press and how he admired anyone who managed to be independent in the current climate. Dad didn't say anything else either. He watched Sandor pouring more wine. Later on he came out with me to clear away the dessert plates and make the coffee. By now everyone had decamped to the front end of the living room where Sandor was making up the fire, presumably to save Dad the bother, or perhaps the shape of the flames didn't suit him. We stood either side of the kitchen table and looked at one another:

Dad: Who the hell is he?

Clay: What, apart from someone who works with Mum?

Dad: I'm surprised he finds the time. He's been in publishing, education, marketing, cat food . . .

Clay: I missed that. Tinned or kibbled?

Dad: Advertising – as soon as he finds out what anyone's job is he starts expounding knowledgeably about it, as if he'd been there too.

Clay: (Still annoyed that this strange man who none of us know has been sitting where my dad should be sitting) I don't like people who talk about themselves all the time.

Dad: No, be fair, he doesn't talk about himself at all. He just makes it impossible for anyone else to talk. Even his wife couldn't get a word in edgeways. I believe she's a secretary but to

	hear him you'd think she was the managing director.
Clay:	What does Mum see in him?
Dad:	Nothing, I hope. I've never heard her singing his praises. I think she wanted them to meet a few people because they're new to the area. God forbid that she likes him so much we have to see them regularly. *The Man Who Came to Dinner*.
Clay:	Sounds like a whodunnit.
Dad:	It's a movie about a terrible guest who breaks his hip on the way out and his hosts are stuck with him. Nineteen forty-one, directed by William Keighly.
Clay:	Have we got it? Shall we try it on them?
Dad:	I was thinking more of *Casablanca* for Mr Harker. 'Of all the gin joints in all the towns in all the world, he walks into mine.'

'I hear you do a paper round,' Sandor Harker said to me when I was changing CDs again, me on the floor, him on the sofa, looking down. I don't often get looked down at.

'How did you hear that?'

'You were telling someone that you'd have to go to

bed soon because of needing to get up early.'

He must have directional receivers.

'Tell me about it.'

'Well, I deliver papers,' I said. 'That's about it, really.'

'Do you do it because you need the money or is it something about being out and about and alone in the early morning?'

I saw why everyone else had been paying so much attention to him. He sounded really interested and understanding. And he was right about the reason I did it. I wondered if he was going to tell me that as well as all the other things he had done, he had once been a paper boy.

'I did a milk round in the vacations, when I was an undergraduate,' he said. 'There is something magical about being out and at work before anyone else, especially in summer, just before the sun comes up. There's something about the light, like being there at the dawn of the world. You must be a morning person, like me.'

I knew what he meant, only I'd never have said it myself, not to someone else. And I didn't imagine that the postmen and milkmen feel very magical, not if it's a full-time job. 'I like it in winter even better,' I said. 'I like being out in the dark.'

'On cold and frosty mornings, Orion sinking in the west, the new moon with the old moon in her arms—'

'Not in the morning,' I said. 'It's the other way round, old moon with the new moon in her arms. I don't even mind if it's raining.'

'What do you mean about the moon?' He frowned; he was really puzzled, or else he didn't like people putting him right, or he wasn't used to it.

'A waxing crescent sets in the evening – that's the new moon with the old moon in her arms. It's the waning crescent you see in the mornings.'

'I never knew that. How can you tell the difference?'

'The horns – the cusps. New moon points to the east, old moon to the west.'

'You're amazing!' he said. He turned to Penny Iverson who was sitting next to him on the sofa. 'Isn't she amazing? How many people do you know who could tell you that?'

I thought Penny probably knew lots of people but he wasn't really asking her, he was too busy being amazed. All the same, it was nice talking to someone who, even if he didn't really find you absolutely fascinating, could make you feel that he did. It wasn't often that people tried to make me feel fascinating – boys, I mean. They could see that they weren't going to get anything out of it and most of the time I felt like one of those film actresses who had to stand in a hole for the love scenes while the short-arse hero stood on a box. But everything about Sandor Harker seemed to be saying, 'I do enjoy talking to you. I really do find you most interesting.'

As he was obviously like that with everyone, I didn't take it personally, which was just as well because even in the pause before Penny started to answer, he seemed to lose interest.

It was Ali laughing that did it. She was standing by the glass doors with Gran and John Iverson. They were fiddling about with coffee cups and talking, and somebody, probably Gran, said something that made Ali laugh. It wasn't loud, but she sort of laughed all over, right down to her feet, as if she was covered in sequins and the movement made them shimmer. Sandor sat forwards and stared at her, then he got up and went over to them leaving Penny still answering the non-question.

For a moment I thought, How lovely, he can't bear not to be with her, but a few moments after that everything had changed. Sandor was talking and everyone was laughing and Ali was staring at him with those Betty Boop eyes again. After a bit they came back and sat down, Sandor on the sofa and Ali on the floor at his feet.

It was after eleven. I knew I'd regret it tomorrow if I didn't go to bed now. As I got up Sandor touched my arm.

'You're stooping. Don't stoop. Be proud of your height.'

He said it in a sort of caressing voice, as if he cared terribly that I might be self-conscious about being the biggest person in the room after him. I didn't know whether to be touched or insulted. Then I noticed Ali nestled down against his knee with her head almost tucked under his jacket, like a little bird under a big bird's wing. I didn't take it in until I was out of the room, but afterwards I remember thinking, But she's grown up. She may be small but she's grown up, she's got a job. Not so long ago Rosie would have snuggled up to Dad like that, but even at eleven Rosie had already reckoned that she was too old and hard to be Daddy's girl. When I looked back on that scene I always pictured Ali sucking her thumb. She wasn't, but she might just as well have been.

Jamze and Rosie had a room each in the attic. This was an ideal arrangement because they despised each other so much that they never spoke, much less argued. I was on the first floor, the same level as Gran and Dad and Mum and the bathroom which is next to mine. I'm a heavy sleeper, constant traffic in and out of the bathroom never disturbs me, but at some point after midnight I was jolted awake by a voice yelling just outside my door.

'This is wonderful! Just like an hotel!'

It was so loud that I thought there was someone in the room and sat bolt upright, groping for the light switch. Then another voice said, 'Sssh,' and there were manly giggles.

It was Sandor out on the landing. He wasn't really yelling, he'd probably forgotten that anyone might be asleep nearby, but he had a carrying voice.

The *sssh* had been female.

I heard him descending the stairs. 'Brilliant idea – we should have one – this is a fabulous house . . . etc . . . etc.' dying away as he went down.

I realized he'd discovered the Cona machine. We keep it on the landing next to the bathroom. There's a timer to switch it on for me at five thirty and we keep it going all day at weekends. It saves trips to the kitchen. It had been there for as long as I could remember, I took it for granted, like the rest of the house, which is hardly fabulous. It was not so brilliant, I thought, that you had to wake everyone up to tell them.

I wondered who the woman had been, warning him to be quiet; Mum, Gran, Penny, Ali even? Typical, I thought afterwards, that Sandor should have been the only one who was audible; the one who woke me up.

Two

Weekends are my least favourite days for delivering papers, partly because the papers are so heavy and partly because my cunning plan does not work. No one else (except Dad) is up even by the time I get back and there on the mat are *our* weekend papers, delivered by someone else from a different shop, and the first thing anyone does is go through them and chuck out the bits that no one's going to read, the financial and travel supplements, the brochures and charity leaflets.

It makes me think of all those people I've been delivering to throwing out hefty chunks of the papers that I've had to carry. I love those scenes in American movies where paper boys cycle down wide suburban streets *hurling* the newspapers in the general direction of front doors; love and envy them. I once weighed the Saturday *Guardian* on the kitchen scales – 987 grammes – but a lot of them are heavier than that, all those colour supplements with special features.

The morning after the party I came in and heard washing-up noises from the kitchen. At that time, on a Saturday? Illogical. I went through and found Dad at the sink. He looked as if he was standing in front of a backdrop of the New York skyline. Against the light coming through the window were little towers; crockery, saucepans, serving dishes . . . last night's washing-up. I'd never seen the kitchen like this. One of the house rules is that washing-up is *never* left till the morning, even after parties, because it is bad for morale. Especially after parties, especially for persons with hangovers. It was definitely bad for morale at that moment. Dad was leaning against the sink, staring out of the window. He looked as if his morale had been left out in the rain and someone had wrung it dry.

He glanced round and saw that it was me – who else would it be at that hour? – and stayed slumped. If it had been Rosie or even Jamze a voice in his head would have bawled, 'Lights! Camera! Action!' A phantom clapperboard would have snapped before his eyes and he'd have gone into Cheery-Dad mode, ready with a joke. He'd have done it for me once, but now we were on the same level it was quite pointless for him to put on an act. I was no longer his little girl and he was the tired man who is actually nearer to Gran's age than Mum's.

He looked especially tired that morning, as if he hadn't had much sleep. All he said, though, was, 'We're going to have to get a dishwasher.'

The reason that we didn't have a dishwasher is that the kitchen is quite small and there really isn't anywhere to put one and with four able-bodied adults in the house (discount Jamze and Rosie) it would have been an unwarranted expense (I quote) although we could easily afford it.

Gran: A dishwasher? How do you think we managed in the Dark Ages?

Dad: I know how *you* managed. You had servants.

Gran: A live-in couple. It wasn't my fault.

Dad: That's why you ran off to live in a tepee in Wales – to dissociate yourself from the plutocracy?

Mum: It was a caravan in Shropshire.

Dad: Only people who grew up with all mod cons think it's romantic to live like peasants.

Gran: Just because you had an outside loo—

Dad: Outside loo? Luxury. We *lived* in an outside loo – fifteen of us. We took turns to sleep in the cistern.

That morning, though, I could see the charms of a dishwasher. 'What happened?'

'We didn't get to bed till three. Penny forgot about driving and was so stewed they had to take a cab home after all. Everyone got stewed. Marina skinned up, fetched her guitar and played Bob Dylan covers. *Desolation Row* at two in the morning – when life is at its lowest ebb. I looked death in the face.'

'What about the Harkers?'

'Walked home, or crawled. The pocket wife was so out of it the front steps must have looked like the north face of the Eiger.'

Pocket wife I liked. I remembered her baby bird impression under Sandor's sheltering wing. 'Did they have far to go?'

'They live up Addington Road, I think,' Dad said, and muttered, as he turned back to the sink, 'Not far enough.'

I wasn't sure that I was supposed to hear that.

'I wonder if they're on my round. I could find out what papers they take. Suppose it turns out that Sandor reads the *Daily Sport*.'

'Sandor submits articles to the *Financial Times* and the *Economist*,' Dad said. 'That's what he turned out to be, an economist, or at least, that's what he gave us to understand. He didn't say whether they get published or not. There's nothing to stop *me* submitting articles to the *FT*, come to that.'

Without saying anything we had started on the New York skyline, Dad doing things properly, glassware first, then cutlery. There were broken glasses on the window sill. I got out three clean tea towels as I could see that one would be inadequate, and started to dry.

'Where would he get a name like Sandor?'

'Must have Hungarians in his back story. Everyone turns out to be Hungarian in the end. Robert Capa – the photographer, Houdini, Leslie Howard, quintessential English actor, most of the British film industry in the Thirties and Forties.'

'Are Hungarians more of a threat to world peace than Canadians?'

'Canadians are undercover Hungarians. It's all in the Bible Code.'

We'd finished the washing-up by the time anyone else put in an appearance and everything was tidied away. The broken glasses were in a jiffy bag so as to protect the binmen from harm.

'Can you face the living room yet?' I asked.

'I have faced it,' Dad said. 'Who do you think

cleared the table? I was too tired to sleep so I got up again when you went out. I'm going down to the studio now to watch *Hurry Sundown*.'

Which meant he was going to catch up on lost sleep. He reckons that *Hurry Sundown* is the most boring film ever made. He saw it in the cinema back in the Sixties and he was just getting ready to leave when he thought the end was coming, and then 'Intermission' flashed up on the screen and he realized it was only half over, so he left anyway. Now he uses it to bore himself to sleep; he still hasn't seen it all the way through. I've never tried it myself; I don't have any trouble sleeping.

The living room smelled of substances so I opened the windows at both ends in spite of the chill. Dad had even cleaned out the fireplace. From the back window I could see down to the studio. The lights were off but the interior was lit by a tell-tale flickering that susceptible people might have taken for signs of paranormal activity. *Hurry Sundown* was already screening and Dad, if there was any justice, was already dozing.

Around mid-morning, by which time I was half-way through my homework, I heard a movement on the landing and feeble fumblings at the coffee machine which I had thoughtfully charged with an extra-strong brew. I'd put out some paracetamol too in case there was a run on the bathroom cabinet.

When I looked out Mum was groping at the Cona jug. I took it away from her because it was scalding hot and full, and poured a mug.

'A dash of milk.'

'Black,' I said meaningly and waved the paracetamol about. 'Take this now, you'll be glad you did later.'

'I didn't wake you up, did I?'

'Wake me up? It's half past ten. Look, daylight. Birds are singing, sun's shining . . .'

'I must have looked at my watch upside-down. Oh God, this is awful, there's all the washing-up to do. No one was in a fit state last night.'

'You mean this morning. Don't worry about the washing-up, we've done it.'

'We?'

'Me and Dad. Sounds like it was quite a party.'

'It was, actually. I can't remember having such a good time for ages.' Mum was nipping at the coffee. She looked at me over the rim of the mug, eyes smiling. 'Bless you for washing up. I wondered where Roger had gone.'

'He got up after me. *And* he's cleaned out the living room,' I said severely. 'Now he's in the studio – *Hurry Sundown*.'

'Hurry what?'

'Sundown. It's the tape he uses for getting to sleep.' The movie jokes are mainly between me and Dad but it hadn't struck me that she wouldn't even know about that one. She was staring past me along the landing.

'I never noticed that before. Look – how extraordinary.'

I looked.

'The pattern on the wallpaper. In this light it seems to be slowly crawling up the wall.'

The wallpaper was doing what it usually does: not very much. What she thought it was doing had nothing to do with the light.

'Optical illusion,' I said. 'You've got a hangover, go back to bed.'

'I never have hangovers. What day is it?'

'Last night was Friday.' I set her on course for the bedroom, leaving her to work it out.

The next time I heard someone at the Cona it was Gran. I knew because she was whistling through her teeth, the only one of us who does whistle. She doesn't do tunes, it's just to prove that they aren't dentures. 'All my own teeth. Pheeeeeeeeeeep!' This was a cheery little number, probably something by Dylan about World War III. It was followed by World War IV in the bathroom; Rosie and Jamze had arisen at the same moment and were fighting in the doorway, so now I knew at least that everyone was alive, while down in the garden studio Dad slept on. Something felt out of synch. Our family routines are not noticeable to the naked eye but they *are* routines and what I was accustomed to, even after late nights, was this: I get up and go out. Dad gets up and goes to studio. Mum gets up. Gran gets up. Jamze and Rosie get up. And yes, it had all happened in the right order, but not in the right way. I wish I'd taken action then, put my considerable foot down, assembled the lemurs and marmosets and told them to get their act together. Then I would have caught the eye of Gran, my fellow primate, over their heads:

Clay: You're supposed to set an example.
Gran: I do. It's greatly to your parents' credit that nobody follows it.
Clay: I know you had a wild youth . . .
Gran: I had several wild youths, heh, heh.

Unfortunately your grandfather wasn't one of them.

Clay: But you really shouldn't be at the draw with Jamze around. He'll be starting on his own before long.

Gran: (Scandalized) You mean he hasn't already? (Self-righteous) Anyway, I never smoke anything in front of the children.

Clay: Jamze is not a child, he's nearly fifteen and his voice is breaking. Anyway, he knows what the fragrance is.

Gran: Don't tell me *you* haven't been toking behind the bike sheds.

Clay: I haven't, actually. The smell turns me up.

Gran: (Pouncing) Ha! You've tried it, then.

Clay: Of course I have.

We never actually had this conversation but we easily could have done. That's how we got along, there wasn't anything we couldn't say to each other. I ought to have said something then. I wish I had.

Lunchtime came and went. Rosie had gone out with friends, Jamze had made himself brunch when I went down – I could tell by the crumbs and other fragments.

Jamze has never really understood the washing-up rule; the part he doesn't understand is that it applies to him. I refilled the landing Cona, since it had been *drained* and all the paracetamol had gone, and wondered if anyone had made coherent plans about dinner. Down in the studio Dad was still out of it – I went and looked through the window. *Hurry Sundown* had ended but it was on a 240 tape, long play. The second feature, *Plan 9 from Outer Space*, was also over and it was on to something I didn't recognize, with animals, probably a wildlife programme from before the days of integrated digital. Dad would wake up to elephants mating or lions chewing their way through a live wildebeest.

As I was coming up the garden Jamze leaned out of the kitchen door and growled (his voice hadn't quite finished breaking so he growled to be on the safe side), 'There's some bloke at the door with flowers.'

'Selling them?'

'Dunno. He asked if Mum was in.'

'What did you tell him?' But Jamze had dragged himself indoors again. He was plugged into his Walkman and once his head was turned he could not see that I was still speaking to him. In addition I could hear Premier League noises from the telly through the still open window of the living room. Whoever the bloke with the flowers was I guessed that Jamze had left him on the step, with the door open. We don't get many door-to-door salesmen and those we do are mostly bent. By now the bogus florist would have whipped inside, rifled handbags and left the premises with the CD player under his coat. He could have nicked the telly from before Jamze's very eyes and Jamze would not have noticed unless it was showing something that kept him awake.

When I got to the front door there was the bloke parked in the porch as I'd suspected, holding a bouquet. It wasn't just a bunch of flowers, it was one of those rustic-bower affairs done up with hessian and hairy string, the way peasant flower arrangers do it in their wattle-and-daub hovels. The flowers were strange lumpy things like mutant thistles and daisies, mixed in with branches of leaves and twiddly twigs. I was mentally pricing it – I knew how much those twiddly twigs alone cost, we got some for Christmas once – when I clocked that the bloke, whom Jamze of course had never met before, was Sandor Harker. He didn't look as if he'd been up till three in the morning. I wondered if he had Ali, the pocket wife, concealed about his person.

'Clay!' he cried, he really did, as though I was the one person he most wanted to see.

I said, 'Sorry about Jamze. He might have asked you in.'

He took this as an invitation to come in anyway.

'Is that your brother?'

'We don't talk about it. He said you wanted Mum.'

Ought I to tell him she was still sleeping it off?

'I brought her these as a thank-you – from us both,' he added.

'I expect Jamze thought you were delivering them,' I said. 'Not that that's any kind of an excuse. I'll put them in water.'

'No need,' he said, 'they're in some sort of solution. All you need is a receptacle. That way you don't have to unwrap them.'

I took the bouquet from him and inside the sacking was a polythene bag full of liquid that moved in my hand. I remember thinking, Is that what breast implants feel like?

'I expect there's a *receptacle* in the kitchen,' I said, noticing that he was closing the door behind him. Wasn't it my place to do that? I still hadn't actively invited him in but he followed me down the hall and the steps to the kitchen and stood in the doorway while

I rooted under the sink for a receptacle, which made me think of chamber pots but was only Sandor-speak for something to put other things in.

'Is Anna at home?'

'Everyone's having a bit of a lie-in,' I said hollowly, my head under the sink where I was reaching to the back for something solid enough to support the bouquet.

'Except you?'

'The paper round.' It would be tactless to mention Dad and the washing-up. I found a heavy stoneware bowl left over from Gran's days as a hippy-type potter, decorated with phallic symbols which fortunately are so symbolic that few people associate them with penises. Coming out backwards I banged my head on the underside of the sink.

In a flash Superman was at my side, all concern, all hands.

'That must have hurt, here, let me . . .' he took the phallic bowl '. . . don't stand up too quickly. Are you seeing stars?'

'Hardly felt it,' I said, which was true. I have thick, tough hair, the sort that grows on Texas Longhorns, but just for a second it was nice to have someone bigger than me making a fuss. Only for a second.

'I'm all *right*.' I clawed my way upright via the draining board and I knew I sounded grumpy. Sandor still had a supporting hand under my elbow, but I didn't really need it or want it. His other hand was feeling the back of my head.

'I think you've got a bump coming.'

'It'll go down again.'

At that moment Jamze came into the kitchen, glanced in our direction long enough to see if I was being molested and decide that even if I was there was no call for him to intervene, and went to the fridge. Sandor sprang away from me as though he really had been caught in the act, which did catch Jamze's attention. He stood gazing at us over the door of the fridge.

'This is Mr Harker,' I said. 'He came to dinner last night. The flowers are for Mum.'

Jamze said 'Unh,' and sank out of sight again because frankly he didn't care what anyone else got up to. After a minute he emerged, gnawing the corner off a litre carton of orange juice, and slouched out again.

The sac of liquid fitted into the bowl even if the whole thing looked dangerously top-heavy.

'Let me carry that for you,' Sandor said chivalrously,

since it was obvious that I was not suffering from a cranial haemorrhage and needed no more TLC.

'I'll leave it in here for now. Mum can decide where she wants it. What are they called – the flowers?'

'Proteas,' he said.

'All of them? They're all different.'

'That's why they're called proteas,' he said, 'after the Roman sea god Proteus who could assume many different forms. Do you do Latin?'

'I dropped it in Year Ten. I want to do politics, history and economics at A level.'

'You ought to meet my son,' Sandor said. 'He's standing for election. I look forward to being able to boast of a family connection in parliament.'

I wouldn't have thought Ali was old enough to have a son old enough to be an MP. He could see what I was thinking.

'By my first wife.'

What was I supposed to say? Is she dead? Are you divorced? My son . . . my first wife . . . didn't these people have names? I just said, 'I'll go and see if Mum's up. Do you want some coffee?'

Now he was looking out of the window, rapt, like stout Cortez on his peak in Darien. 'What a lovely garden. Oh – you've got a shed.'

'It's Dad's studio. Do you want some coffee?'

'No, it's a shed. Every man should have a shed.'

'Have you got one?' I didn't mean to sound rude, questioning his manhood, but I still hadn't got an answer. Perhaps I was phrasing it wrong. 'Would you like me to make you a cup of coffee?'

'You know how it is with men and sheds. No, I won't stop for a coffee if Anna's still in bed. You must have lots to do.'

'I did, but I've done it.'

At last he made up his mind and headed back along the hall. I let him out and he stood in the porch looking down at me searchingly.

'Do take care of that head.'

'I've got a spare,' I said, but quietly, and not until he had turned to go down the steps.

'Who was that?' Almost before I'd got the door shut there was Mum on the stairs, looking half awake in a decadent way in her floaty dressing gown that she calls a peignoir. It's transparent, whatever it is, but at least she had a nightie under it. 'I thought I heard a man's voice.'

'You might have put something decent on, then,' I said, 'unless you were planning to seduce him.'

'Oh, don't be a prude. I was coming down anyway.

Bless you for letting me sleep. Who was it?'

'Sandor Harker, from last night – I mean, he came round to thank you for last night. They've sent you flowers.'

'Oh, they shouldn't have bothered.'

'No, they should have given them to me and Dad. Hint, hint.'

'Oh.' She did look guilty. 'The washing-up. I'll make it up to you.'

'Make it up to Dad, he cleaned up as well – and the fireplace.'

'Do you know, I feel disgustingly mellow,' she said, sashaying round the newel post. The peignoir has flounces. 'And very hungry. Is there anything for lunch?'

'Jamze and Rosie ate the leftovers. I could do you an omelette.'

She was on the kitchen steps by now, coming face to face with the proteas on the draining board.

'What on earth—'

'That's what Sandor brought. A bit over the top, if you ask me. They look more like botanical specimens than flowers.'

The doorbell rang. I turned back to answer it, leaving her to admire the bouquet. I didn't recognize the woman in the porch for a moment, all I took in was that she was clutching a bunch of flowers. I couldn't see what they were except that they must be quite small and normal, by the size of the wrapping paper.

She said, 'Hullo, Clay.'

It was Ali Harker, and I hadn't recognized her because standing up, on her own, she didn't look all that tiny even from my high ground, nothing of the pocket wife about her, even without *him* to measure her against. She was wearing jeans and a sweater, as if last night's gloss had just been reflected off him, and without make-up she didn't have that airbrushed look of careful perfection. She was just, well, lovely, because she was happy, I suppose. I never saw her looking quite like that again.

I hadn't liked her at all last night because she'd hardly been there *to* like, just a sort of shiny appendage, like an earring. But now, I saw, in those few seconds, here was someone you'd love to have as a friend because you'd always feel good when she was around. I wasn't aware of feeling any of this at the time; all I was thinking was, *More* flowers.

She held them out. 'I brought these for Anna. I feel

awful about last night, we kept you all up so late . . .'

'You didn't keep *me* up,' I said. 'Come in,' and as I said it I had a premonition of what was going on behind me, only it was too late to do anything about it. As Ali stepped over the threshold Mum came down the hall with the proteas.

'Oh, wow!' Ali said. 'Those are amazing.'

I'd taken her bunch from her. It was yellow roses and gypsophela, nothing special but pretty, and the roses were scented.

'Ali!' Mum hadn't recognized her either, at first. 'You shouldn't have. They're beautiful.'

Ali was trying to work it out. She knew Mum couldn't be talking about the roses because she hadn't seen them yet. I was still closing the door.

'Sorry?' she said.

'It was a lovely thought. I'm putting them in the front room where they'll catch the sun.'

'Sandor brought them round,' I said, hoping to get things sorted quickly.

'Sandor? Brought those? Brought them here?' She was looking at the proteas which might as well have had a ticket on them declaring, 'PURCHASED AT VAST AND UNNECESSARY EXPENSE', and at Mum, all dishevelled in her see-through peignoir – *déshabillé* is the correct word, I think – and putting two and two together.

'Sandor was here? But I told him . . .' Her hand was starting to wave about. I put the roses in it. 'I said I'd be . . .' She smiled, bravely. 'We must have got our wires crossed.'

I wished I'd kept my mouth shut. I wanted to reassure her: 'Don't worry, he didn't even see Mum,' but I'd said too much already. And Mum, who hadn't a clue what was going on, said, 'And roses too? Oh, Ali, what a lovely thought. Clay, put them in water. Can you stay for coffee?'

Ali was still staring at the proteas. I didn't have a clue what was going on either; did she?

'No, I won't stay,' Ali said. 'Must get back. I just wanted to thank you for a lovely evening. It's our turn next – I'll ring you.'

As I let her out it was starting to come together. I didn't believe for a moment that there had been any crossed wires. I had a nasty feeling that Sandor had known perfectly well that Ali was going to bring flowers, nice ordinary flowers that ordinary people give each other to say thank you, and had got in first with his monster bunch.

Why would he do that? All sorts of clips flashed

before my eyes: Mum getting up five minutes earlier and Ali arriving to find her and Sandor together; the peignoir; me being elsewhere. I still didn't know what was going on, but I didn't like it.

At four o'clock I made a sandwich and took it down to Dad in the studio. The tape should be about finished, I calculated, and I didn't want to leave him any longer in case he couldn't sleep that night.

I timed it perfectly. The credits were rolling, gaffers, grips, best boys, with names you couldn't make up; Ulik Earfahrt and Mince Bordello. Dad was awake:

Dad: Have I missed anything?

Clay: Some big ugly flowers arrived with Sandor
        Harker attached.

Dad: Well, they would have to be big, wouldn't
        they?

Clay: And then the pocket wife, who is quite large
        on her own, brought some roses round to
        thank us for last night.

Dad: Overkill. We only gave them dinner.

Clay: I'm not sure that's all we gave them.

Dad: Meaning?

Clay: We seem to have given Sandor ideas. I'll swear

he knew Ali was bringing roses. And he was all over me when I banged my head on the sink, and then when Jamze came in . . .

This is not the conversation we had. I'd more or less planned it but I could see where it would lead. Dad would get ideas too; the wrong ideas about Sandor. I didn't know what the right idea was, but I didn't want Dad thinking that Sandor had been trying to molest me, because I hadn't got the impression that Sandor was the least interested in doing anything of the sort. I was just a sort of stage property for him to do things with. Dad knew I was unlikely to be at risk – he was the only one who hadn't protested about the paper round – but he would have felt that he ought to do something about it, naturally, and I wasn't sure what *it* was. So when Dad said, 'Have I missed anything?' I just told him, 'Well, everyone finally got up although Gran has been in the bathroom for fifty minutes and may have drowned, and the Harkers have given us some flowers to thank us for last night.'

'Us,' Dad said, 'or Anna?'

'The hostess.'

'Trust the menials to get overlooked. They might have left us a tip.'

'What were you watching?'

'No idea. Marina would have liked it. I woke up ten minutes before the end – there was some sort of werewolf running about in Wal-Mart. Big shoot-out round the canned-fish gondola. I'll run it back later and check the title. What are your plans for the evening?'

'I'm going round to Daisy's to revise.'

'On a Saturday night? What kind of life is that for a growing girl?'

'It might stunt my growth, with luck,' I said. 'Anyway, I'm stopping over. We'll let rip late into the night.'

Saturday was the one night of the week I didn't have to get to bed early. Sunday papers are delivered later on the assumption that everyone is having a lie-in. Even the Mirzas don't open up till six thirty. It did seem a pity to spend it revising but we had GCSEs looming up. (Daisy was only free because she and her boyfriend had dumped each other simultaneously and now she was having a twenty-four-hour humiliation because she'd thought *he* would be licking his wounds). Sandor had been so not interested in my A level plans. I'd have thought an economist might have something to say to someone who was planning to study economics, but he'd just led off about his high-flying (nameless) son.

Still, he had told me to be proud of my height. Perhaps he'd been trying to be kind. It would have been kinder not to mention it.

Three

The proteas lasted for ages. I'd hoped that being so big and showy they'd die soon, like lilies, but they stayed exactly the same. The twiddly twigs put out leaves. In the end Mum stuck them into a flower bed to see if they'd root (they did) so that we'd have free twiddly twigs at Christmas for evermore, and Gran hung the proteas upside down in the back lobby to dry out. Even dry they didn't look any different.

Ali's gyp and roses died a natural death.

I assumed that Sandor was still at DDI as he'd only just joined it, but Mum never mentioned him and although the proteas, drying in the lobby, had a significance, I didn't think about the Harkers much.

Except, occasionally, coasting down Addington Road in the mornings, I'd wonder which was their house. I knew I didn't deliver to it because I'd checked. Mr Mirza has something like a horn book for each of his deliverers, with addresses pasted on and the names of the papers that go with them. I looked in the receipt book but none of the Addington Road addresses belonged to Harker. Most of the houses down there are like ours, tall narrow semis with a cellar or an attic, or sometimes both, but a few are detached, with ornate woodwork round the porches, and big gardens. I could imagine Ali gardening, looking like Felicity Kendall in *The Good Life*, but Sandor? Sandor, I thought, would probably grow orchids or bromeliads or, at the other extreme, giant redwoods.

Wherever they lived, they were never about at ten to seven when I went by. In summer, on bright mornings, I'd look at all those bedroom windows with closed curtains and wonder how anyone can bear to be in bed after it gets light. I never sleep with the curtains drawn. I remember how I used to hate it when I was little and had to go to bed before it got dark. Mum drew the curtains but I could still see the light coming in round them and got all tight with resentment because I was wasting it. This was when I was still at the 'It's not fair!' stage. Then one evening I just got up and opened the curtains. In the morning Mum looked at them and said, 'I didn't forget to draw them, did I?' Honest Clay said, 'No, I did it, I don't like being in the dark when it's light.' 'But you won't be able to sleep, darling.' 'But I did sleep,' I pointed out. She never drew the curtains again.

And then the invitation came. This makes it sound as if it was engraved on deckle-edged card with 'Black tie' at the bottom like the one that came when Dad got the design award, that strange resin shape on a plinth that he keeps by the studio door to brain passing crims who have been known to leg it across the garden on their way to the allotments.

The Harkers' invitation was just an ordinary card with Monet's *Water Lilies* on it, but it seemed formal because most of our social arrangements are made by phone. They were having a party, 'From three pm until it ends.' There was something girlie about that but I didn't think it had come from Ali. Whoever did write it had added, 'Why don't you all come?'

'Do they know how many "all" adds up to?' Dad said. 'Does it include Jamie and Rosie? Are they aware that Jamie and Rosie exist?'

'Of course they are,' Mum said. 'Well, Sandor knows how many children I have.'

'Can you see Jamie partying with the Harkers?' Dad said. 'He'll make straight for the telly.'

I could see Rosie partying. Rosie is a party of one. She wouldn't care who the other guests were so long as they made a backdrop for Rosie's glitz and bling from Claire's Accessories.

'Well, ask them,' Gran said.

'Are we asking me?' I said.

'Don't you want to come?' Mum said.

I didn't know whether I wanted to or not. My experiences of parties then was hanging around gloomily on the fringes watching other people snog, fighting off the ones who wanted to snog me because I was still available and therefore, they calculated, desperate enough to want them, and ending up in the kitchen with some other no-hoper who would sidle up and confess to me that he thought he was gay. I hated the confession part. Why couldn't they just say, 'I don't fancy you. I'm gay.' Then I realized that what they were confessing was that they weren't sure. I used to think, Well, can't you tell? – but lately I'd been wondering, Perhaps I am, too. Why don't I surrender to one of these hopeful snoggers instead of wiping them off before they even get their tongues out? Daisy told me, 'People are calling you a Lezzie,' but then I thought, Well, maybe I am, but why don't I fancy any of my girl friends? That's the clincher, surely. Preferring women. 'Probably a late developer,' Daisy said. She meant well.

But this party obviously would not be at all like that and anyway, I was really curious to see the house because, naturally, there was an address for RSVP. It turned out to be my favourite house in the whole of Addington Road, one I'd always wondered about the inside of. The road makes a dogleg just there, where it was extended during the 1930s, and the Harkers' house was right on the bend; big, detached, with a garden all round it – you could see trees over the side hedge – and its porch was built into the corner. It had a white wooden railing round two sides and above it was a balcony, also railed, with plant pots. It was my dream house, I used to picture myself sitting on that balcony, being able to look up and down the road. Of course, at ten to seven in the morning there was never anyone on it. I would have been, at all hours. I'd noticed it going up for sale and being sold quite quickly – one week there was a Renault outside the garage, the next an Audi, left-hand drive. I'd half thought of having a poke around the garden if it stood empty, but I never got the chance. I couldn't pass it up now.

'It's not going to be a formal affair,' Mum said, 'but the weather's so good now they thought that with luck they could start with tea in the garden and then carry on from there. Anyone can leave at any time.'

'No one on the exit with a sub-machine gun, then,' Gran said.

Rosie instantly arranged a sleepover with a friend. Jamze's grunt was interpreted as 'Jolly kind of you to ask, old bean, but thank you, no,' so it was going to be the usual suspects; Mum, Dad, me and Gran:

Clay: You're going to leave the guitar at home, aren't you?

Gran: I'm thinking of taking up the saxophone. It's the instrument of choice for girls these days.

Dad: Because of Bill Clinton?

Gran: Because of Lisa Simpson.

Clay: Are you going to write a reply?

Mum: No, I'll phone.

Dad: Can't you just tell him?

Mum: I will if I see him.

Clay: Send a card. I'll deliver it.

Pathetic, really, but every time I'd passed that house, number 107, I'd wished that I could deliver papers to it so I could walk up the six steps to the porch, past the railing to the door. I'd noticed, in a professional way, that their letter box was very large. Half the time I was trying to ram wads of newsprint the size of a bloomer loaf through slits dating from Edwardian times when letters were little dainty things. Then there are the idiots whose letter flaps are at the bottom of the door so that you practically have to go down on your hands and knees to get anything through. My heart goes out to postmen, it really does.

Mum wrote a reply, giving numbers, on another card with some more of Monet's water lilies, or the same water lilies from a different angle, and left it by the landing Cona for me to collect, so *that* morning I finally got to climb the six steps to the porch of 107 and had a sneak preview of the Harkers' living room because one of the windows overlooks the porch. The curtains were open and I could see into what was obviously an L-shaped living room with french windows opposite, and heavy antique-looking furniture and heavy antique-looking books. Then from behind the front door I heard a voice calling out. The milk was still on the step, two pints of semi-skinned and two of orange juice. Someone might open the door, someone might appear suddenly on the other side of the window, inadequately clad, if they were anything like us. I didn't want anyone to be embarrassed, me included, so I slipped off the porch, out of the gate, onto the bike, and was already pushing away from the kerb when the door opened. From that angle all I caught was a glimpse of a hand reaching down for the bottles. Whoever owned it was probably standing on our envelope at that very moment. Still, neither snow nor rain nor heat nor gloom of night stays this courier from the swift completion of her appointed round. Clay Winchester, ace rider with the Pony Express, urges her mustang on across Monument Valley while the tumbleweeds roll by. Eat my dust, punk.

Rosie threw a strop on the day of the party. If we'd been paying attention we'd have seen her working up to it because Rosie's strops are show-stoppers, big production numbers, and you don't get that kind of effect with improv.

After we'd shoehorned Jamze out of the bathroom she came down from the attic and noticed us doing our usual turn-and-turn-about routine. Timing was perfect – Dad on his way upstairs, Mum going into the bathroom, Gran coming out, me in my doorway:

Dad: My turn next!
Gran: That flush is acting up again.
Mum: You're after me. I'm only going to shower.

Clay: You have to count to three before you let go.

Rosie: (Aggressive) I'll do my homework tomorrow. Right? (Slams down backpack)

Mum: I thought you did it last night.

Rosie: No you didn't. You didn't even *think*.

Dad: (Mild) You ought to get it out of the way before you go over to – to—

Rosie: See! You don't even know where I'm going. I *told* you—

Mum: You told *me*. Stop shouting.

Rosie: (*Fortissimo*) I'm not shouting, you're shouting, I'm sick of shouty people *ignoring* me—

Gran: No one's ignoring you, my little magic mushroom. Chance would be a fine thing.

Rosie: No one asked *you*.

Mum: Go and get it done now, then we can drop you off before we go. And don't speak to Granny like that.

Rosie: That's right, it's all my fault, you'll be late and it'll all be my fault, drop me off, that's all you ever do, get me out of the way before you go off with your weird friends.

Dad: Do your homework *now*. I'll help you if you need it. Go and fetch it—

Rosie: Excuse me? Who said I needed help? Just get

off my case! (Becomes incoherent at this point
and exits, weeping hysterically)

Something like that . . . Read the script and you will
notice that until Rosie came storming down from her
room no one had even mentioned homework, done or
undone. Somebody who didn't know the score would
guess that Rosie, far from being the pampered baby
of the family, was neglected, her schoolwork
unsupervised, left to hang out with bad company who
would lead her astray while the rest of us indulged
ourselves with wild parties and Satanism. What
it boiled down to, in fact, was that she was having
trouble with her maths and wanted someone to help
her only she couldn't bring herself to ask. And if she
was having trouble she didn't see why the rest of us
shouldn't have a bit as well. She's generous like that.

Dad going off to do tessellations or whatever it was,
threw the bathroom rota out of kilter, so I went next
after Mum instead of last which is what I like because
it is more leisurely. But none of us felt leisurely now,
thanks to Rosie. I'd planned a nice soak, hair wash
and time to decide what to wear because I imagined
that Ali would look stunning and I wanted to make
the effort for her sake. If I ever look stunning it is

because I am carrying a blunt instrument – hockey stick, frying pan – but I do have some nice clothes. Now the heart had gone out of it. I just went for the usual look, safe; black trousers and black top, not stretch. Stretch is all right if it isn't stretching.

It felt odd, *walking* to a party in the middle of the afternoon. We looked as if we were out for a stroll which is something families used to inflict on each other, I believe, at weekends, before daytime television. At least we didn't have Rosie whining in the rear. She had already gone off to whichever friends she was staying with, tarted up as if she was the partygoer. I knew how she was going to spend the evening, they'd be painting each other's toenails and braiding each other's hair into what they imagined were corn rows but actually looked more like scar tissue after field surgery, all in a heap on a duvet, like macaques grooming each other for fleas. Jamze had been left in front of the box but I was sure he'd be down the offy as soon as we were out of sight, and texting his mates for an evening of depravity. There'd be a row tomorrow because Jamze had not then learned to cover his tracks.

Mum and Dad walked together, I followed with Gran who was looking majestic in a black tunic over green silk trousers, and a long floaty scarf. She's as tall and broad as I am but she's had longer to get used to it.

'Anyone we know going to be there?' Dad was saying.

'The Iversons,' Mum said. 'People from work – Tim and Mary, Maureen . . .'

I began thinking again that, really, I shouldn't be there. I ought to be in town with *my* friends who wouldn't be seen dead walking around in broad daylight with parents and grandparents. If it all got too horrible I could find a secluded corner and text SOS messages to them: Rng m nw! Smn m 2 ur dthbd!

Or I could do what Rosie would have done, stand in the middle of a group and text away openly so that everyone knew she was rotting from the head down with boredom.

We'd wondered what to bring with us. 'Sandor says it's not a bottle party,' Mum said. 'Well, starting with afternoon tea, it wouldn't be.'

'The proteas are still in good nick,' Gran had said. 'Wrap them up in a bit of onion net and binder twine to look suitably rustic and they may not realize they've seen them before.'

'Ali will,' I said, remembering the awkward scene

in the hall, but only I knew about that because Mum hadn't noticed the awkwardness and no one else had been there.

'We ought to take something,' Dad said, 'because if we don't everyone else will. Sod's Law. Anyway, four of us ... perhaps we could each bear a little home-made gift tied up with tissue paper and pink string.'

'I don't know why we're making such a fuss,' Mum said. 'We don't usually have any trouble.'

'Exactly,' Dad said. 'What would we normally take? A nice chianttttti.'

'Oh, make it a bottle of good champagne and say that it's for them to celebrate with on their own when they've got shot of us all,' Mum said.

Gran remarked, 'I've just read a survey in the paper. Apparently champagne is now the favoured drink of the masses – instead of lager, I suppose. Perhaps a six-pack of Kestrel would be more appropriate.'

We'd settled for a magnum of classy champagne as a mere bottle between the four of us would have looked mean. But I kept thinking of what Dad had said; why did we feel we had to make such a thing of it? After all, we still hardly knew them.

* * *

We could hear the party before we got to the corner, voices and laughter and music.

'They've got a string quartet playing in the gazebo,' Dad said.

'It's only half past three,' Gran said. 'Full house already, by the sound of it. They must have bussed them in, en masse. AA signs on the ring road: "Harker fans this way".'

That was overdoing it, but I almost expected a notice by the side gate with an arrow on it. A high thorn hedge blocked the view into the back garden from the front and the gate was a wooden one that you couldn't see through, but as soon as we set foot on the gravel path the front door started to open. Someone was obviously keeping a lookout.

'They must have sensors,' Dad hissed, 'an infra-red beam across the gateway.'

'Like in *The Fisher King* – no, that was a laser, wasn't it? We should have limboed under it,' I said.

We were both picturing that, so we were falling against each other by the time the door was properly opened by someone who looked oddly familiar.

'You must be the Winchesters,' he said, whoever he was. I thought, How does he know? – and imagined Sandor having given him such a minute description of us that we were instantly recognizable: one small woman, two big women, one average man. 'Come in.'

'And you must be Oscar,' Mum said, and there was a log jam in the hall while she introduced the rest of us. It was obvious from the look of him that this was Sandor's son, the one with political ambitions.

'Oz,' Oscar said and then, when the how-do-you-dos had died down, 'Everyone calls me Oz,' in case we hadn't heard.

'I bet,' Dad muttered, as we were herded through to the garden, 'that everyone calls him Ozzy and makes jokes about biting the heads off bats.'

'Oscar Harker – doesn't really flow, does it?'

'No doubt conceived during the Academy Awards,' Dad said. 'Backstage at Graumann's Chinese Theatre.'

'Good thing it wasn't during the Baftas.'

'Will you two shut up and behave,' Mum said.

I don't know why we were being rude about Oscar because although he looked so much like Sandor he was perfectly nice and perfectly normal, in a way that Sandor was not. He got us out into the garden and made sure we all had food and drink.

'Dear God, buck's fizz and cucumber sandwiches,'

Gran said. 'At this hour. What'll it be like by tonight? I hope they've invited the neighbours.'

There was no string quartet in the gazebo, the music was coming from a sound system by the french windows. There must have been about forty people there and too many children for my liking, all behaving badly, rushing about screaming or – as I'd surmised – calling their friends. Rosie would have been perfectly at home. None of them seemed to be attached to parents, at least, no one was saying 'Don't' or 'Be quiet' or just throwing them over the fence for someone else to clear up. If the Harkers hadn't known anybody when they moved here in March they'd certainly made up for it since.

Mum was talking to the Iversons, Gran had got in with three other Gran-types and they were all under a tree having a crafty fag. Dad had spotted someone he knew and they zoomed in on each other because, clearly, Dad was the only person there that this guy recognized. I didn't know anyone. I did what I always ended up doing at parties, withdrew to the sidelines and held my glass in that way, I've noticed since, people on their own at parties always do: weight on one leg, hand supporting elbow of arm that's holding the drink, looking cool, detached and as miserable as hell.

Oz came over to where I was standing and said, 'Do you know anyone?'

'There's two or three I deliver papers to, but I don't think they know me. They only see me at Christmas when they come out in the dark and give me a tip.'

'I don't either,' Oz said. 'Know any of them.'

'Don't you live here?'

'God, no,' he said. 'I'm only visiting. Do you want to sit down?'

'Yes, but there's nowhere to sit.'

'Should be cushions . . .' he said, looking suddenly irritated. 'Never mind.' And he sat, on the grass, beckoning me down. 'It only takes one – or in our case two . . .' he said as I folded up beside him '. . . and within five minutes everybody follows suit. And once that happens the feral children will calm down too. You watch – oh, there's the door again.'

'How can you tell?' I asked. 'We thought you must have detector rays.'

'Not quite,' he said. 'Sensors in the gateway which activate the security light. I left it switched on, which is why I've been staring over your shoulder instead of gazing into your eyes and engaging you in meaningful conversation. Sorry – back in a minute.'

He wasn't, but it didn't matter so much now because

he'd been right about people sitting down, and about the children. Mum came over with Penny Iverson and gradually we regrouped.

'Don't go too mad with the hooch,' Gran said. 'I've seen what they've got lined up for later.'

'Trust you to go snooping about,' Mum said.

'I went to the loo,' Gran retorted, 'as one does. They've got three, I cased the joint. One by the front door, in the hall, one upstairs and one in the bathroom, if you're interested.'

By this time I'd seen Sandor swooping round the garden telling everyone what a good idea it was to sit on the grass. It would have been a better idea if he'd come out sooner and said it himself instead of leaving it to Oz. All those kitten heels couldn't have been doing his lawn any good. It seemed to be the first time he'd come out because he was welcoming people, and most of them had arrived before we had. While he was still working his way round to us I decided to follow Gran's example. It would be a good opportunity to see what the house was like indoors, so instead of using the downstairs loo I had a quick look round before going up to the first floor.

I'd seen the L-shaped living room from the porch and there was a dining room on the other side of the hall. It was all the same kind of furniture and curtains, heavy and solemn, not old but old-looking, with glum oil paintings, portraits, the sort you'd inherit rather than go out and buy. Very Sandor, but not very Ali, it seemed to me. The kitchen, where all the bottles were lined up on the dresser, was wonderfully big with a long table and more food laid out on it, but I couldn't imagine anyone cooking there. It was more like an imitation kitchen in a catalogue that sells high-class cookware.

Then I went upstairs. The landing ran across the middle of the house with a window at one end and a french door at the other which must be the one that led out on to the balcony over the porch. I went and tried it; I really did want to step out on that balcony, but it was locked. All I could do was admire the begonias in the planters. The carpet was pale – I checked my soles before I stepped on it – the walls were papered cream and light green; it was all airy and unlived-in. I felt as though I ought not to be there but, after all, I was a guest. The loo and bathroom were next to each other. I chose the bathroom because I wanted to see what it was like, and it was just as I expected, clean as a catalogue. Nothing looked as if it had ever been used; not that ours was filthy but no one could ever doubt that it was shared by six careless people who were always in a hurry. To be honest, a casual observer would have guessed twelve careless people.

As I was going in I noticed another open door farther down the landing. I was just sneaking along to put my head round it when behind another door I heard a sound, someone crying.

I thought it was a child at first, got lost, shut in, having a strop like Rosie who, weeping in the attic, can be heard clearly in the kitchen, and I almost went to the door and knocked, almost opened it. Then I realized it wasn't a child, it was a woman, but she was crying like a child, not loud and bawling but quietly, on and on, because it was impossible to stop.

Then I remembered that I still hadn't seen Ali.

I didn't go into the bathroom after all, I ran back down the stairs and used the loo by the front door.

When I went out into the garden I turned left instead of right, round to the other side where the party wasn't happening. It was that bit all gardens have, ours included, with the hose and the compost bin and pot plants that aren't doing very well. I wanted a few minutes to think.

I'd heard something I wasn't supposed to hear. I knew something I wasn't supposed to know. What I couldn't tell was, Am I supposed to do anything about it?

At school if anyone started crying in a cupboard or a cloakroom, there'd be a support group forming within seconds, soothing, hugging, half of them joining in out of solidarity even if they didn't know what it was all about. But this was someone I'd met only twice and hardly knew and anyway, she was a grown-up. I'd stopped thinking of other people as grown-ups quite some while ago, it's a height thing, but just then I was thinking, I don't have to do anything, I'm too young, which was ridiculous but I was looking for a get-out clause.

I wondered what Mum or Gran would have done and whether to tell them. That was ridiculous too, running to the adults: 'Mummy! Granny! There's a lady upstairs crying in the bedroom,' very loudly, the way some children do, so that everyone hears.

Tell Sandor?

He might be the one who'd made her cry.

Who else could it have been?

In the end the sensible idea won which was, How would I feel if it was me and a near-stranger came busting in and told everybody? It must be bad enough feeling that desperate when your home was full of visitors and there was nowhere to hide. That settled it. If I wouldn't like it I was fairly sure Ali wouldn't. What she did in her own house was her own business and it wasn't mine. I went back to the party.

The first person I ran into, coming round the ornamental bamboo by the back door, was Sandor.

'Clay!' That joyful cry again, as if I was the one person he wanted to see. 'Where have you been?'

'I took a wrong turning,' I said.

'I wondered where you'd got to. Anna told me you'd be coming,' he said. 'Have you had a drink? Come and meet some people.'

I didn't tell him that I'd already spent the best part of an hour not meeting people. 'Where's Ali?' I said. 'I haven't seen her yet.'

'Oh, somewhere about. Things got delayed – she hadn't had time to change when people started arriving.'

That must have been about ninety minutes ago, I thought, but before I could even wonder whether to say anything he bounced on.

'Don't you ever wear frocks, Clay?'

Frocks? Frocks make me think of drag acts.

'I'm more a trousers person,' I said. 'Not really built for frocks,' and I also thought he had a nerve even mentioning it. Did he talk like that to all women? To Mum? Probably.

We were still behind the bamboo. He looked at me very seriously. 'You mustn't be self-conscious, Clare. You'd look super in something long and dark.'

'No one calls me Clare,' I said, 'except at school.'

'It's a lovely name. It suits you. Clay sounds so butch. Don't be afraid to be feminine. Tall women can be so graceful.'

That made me feel butch enough to want to take a swing at him.

Someone was coming round the corner to the back door. Sandor leaned forward conspiratorially and put his hand on my shoulder.

'Wear a frock next time, just for me. You'll see – you'll feel quite different.'

Whoever it was edged past us and in at the door as if trying not to notice, and Sandor noticed them too late to do his guilty spring away. The someone else came out and I shrugged him off and went back to the party. I was already thinking, Why did he do that? Just like when Jamze came into the kitchen that time Sandor brought the proteas round. It was almost as if he wanted to be seen pawing and yet it hadn't felt like pawing, more as if he'd known that because he'd been seen he wouldn't have to go any further. I thought, If he ever does that again I'll *fling* myself at him, see what he does then.

The party was getting very relaxed. Some of the worst children had been removed and from just sitting on the grass people were starting to recline on it, propped on one elbow like guests at a Roman banquet. Then I saw Ali coming out through the French windows with Oz. They were carrying piles of rugs and floor cushions. I went over to help, partly because Ali's heap was starting to topple, partly because I wanted to see if she was all right.

It was hard to tell. When she saw who I was she smiled and said hullo and thank you. She was carefully made up but her eyes were bloodshot and she didn't look very happy. Oz looked angry.

I said, 'What are you going to do, drop them among people?'

'I meant to bring them out earlier, before anyone sat down,' Ali said. 'I don't *think* the grass is damp.'

'That's our fault,' I explained. 'Oz said that if we sat down everyone else would.'

'I forgot about this lot.' Oz had the cushions piled

under his chin like a multi-decker burger. I knew *he* hadn't forgotten. Someone else had.

I looked at Ali, all innocent. 'There's so many people here. I didn't see you before.'

'Ah, for a thrash like this there's a lot going on behind the scenes,' Oz said.

I bet there is, I thought. Ali was looking straight past me. Under the tree where the rogue grannies had been smoking, Sandor was talking to Penny Iverson, standing very close. Penny was looking up at Sandor and laughing but she hadn't much choice about looking up, he was almost on top of her. Behind me I heard Oz mutter, 'Leave it, Ali. Leave it.'

It was after six, shadows were lengthening but it was still hot. Sandor was rushing about collecting tea things, and bottles were appearing on the rugs and among the cushions. I said to Mum, 'I think I'll go home now, if you don't mind.'

Mum: Of course I don't mind, but aren't you having a nice time?
Clay: (Lying) Yes, but I've had enough of a nice time.
Dad: I'll come with you.
Mum: Oh, don't tell me you're bored too.

Dad: No, but as our daughter says, enough nice already. You two can stay for the debauch if you like.

Gran: (At work on a Camberwell carrot) We shall.

Dad: But don't be surprised if you get raided. I caught a flash of light more than once from that loft extension over the road. I think someone's up there with binoculars.

Clay: *Rear Window*. James Stewart and Grace Kelly.

Gran: Never seen it. Can't stand Hitchcock.

Dad: Heresy.

Clay: He's probably been keeping the place under surveillance for weeks, laid up with a broken leg . . .

Dad: (Who has had some very robust therapy for lower back problems at the orthopaedic hospital) Wouldn't wash, these days. The physios would have him on his feet as he came out of surgery.

Clay: . . . watching Sandor bury his first wife in the flower bed.

'Do you think we ought to say goodbye to our hosts?' Dad wondered as we left. 'I can't see them.'

Nor could I, but indoors, upstairs, a door slammed.

Then I spotted Oz coming round the bamboo. I was beginning to think of that bamboo as part of a stage set, especially erected to hide behind and eavesdrop in.

'Oz is a sort of host,' I said.

'Who is he again?'

'Sandor's son.'

'Does he know his mother's under the roses?'

'*Dad.*' I went over to Oz before he came over to us and heard what Dad was saying.

'Leaving already?' He didn't sound surprised.

I had a cover story ready. 'Dad's got some work to finish. I said I'd help him. Can you say goodbye to Ali and Sandor for us? I don't know where they are.'

'I'll pass the message on,' Oz said. He smiled, but he was looking deeply gloomy. 'Well, it was nice meeting you, Clay.'

'You too,' I said, and I meant it. In spite of looking so much like his father he was nothing like Sandor in any other way, I felt sure. Poor old Oz, I thought. He's got to stay till the end.

We let ourselves out by the side gate.

'Well, that was a rum do,' Dad said as we crossed the gravel. 'I thought at first it was going to be like one of Gatsby's parties.'

'Whose?'

'*The Great Gatsby*, by F. Scott Fitzgerald. You ought to have read it by now.'

'I've seen the film – I think.'

'It obviously didn't make much of an impression. Read the book, it isn't very long; about a man who throws enormous parties but never shows up at them. He's hoping to lure back the woman he loves, even though she's married someone else. He can't understand that he's lost her for ever.'

'Doesn't sound much like Sandor.'

We swung down the hill in step, as if expecting the bad guys in black hats to come round the corner. It occurred to me that there are very few hills in Westerns. Obviously there are mountains, and the Black Hills of Dakota, and buttes in Monument Valley, but the towns are always built on the flat, unlike European ones that usually started off on high ground for defensive purposes, and very near a river. Rivers figure largely in Westerns, so that people can be picked off while crossing them, but not near towns. You never find out where these pioneers got their water supply.

All this crossed my mind before Dad said, 'Well, Sandor didn't show up for ages.'

'Eh?'

'Like Gatsby. Nor did the pocket wife.'

'She's not that small, actually, when you see her on her own.'

'Perhaps they were enjoying spontaneous passion upstairs.'

I nearly said, 'I don't think that's what they were doing,' but I didn't. I didn't know what to say, feeling almost as embarrassed as if I had walked in on them having passionate sex on the carpet. Instead I said, 'Was there really someone watching from the window over the road?'

'Flight of fancy,' Dad said. 'I saw a woman at the window, but ten minutes later she came down and joined the party.'

'How do you know it was the same woman?'

'That harpy in the screaming pink frock. Once seen, never forgotten.'

Frock. I was never going to like that word.

'And the flashes of light?'

'There was something hanging in the window, a wind chime or crystals. She was probably aligning her chakras.'

I've never been too sure what chakras are. They sound like something Mexican cowhands might wear in cactus country.

*   *   *

I was not very good at the big sister bit. That didn't matter with Rosie because all Rosie needed was a stooge to bounce her tantrums off. If Mum or Gran weren't around to ruin her life I made a useful substitute. None of us needed to do anything ruinous, so it wasn't particularly hard work.

It was different with Jamze. There are five years between me and Rosie, but only fourteen months between me and Jamze (who is in any case a different life form; women are from Venus, men are from Battersea Dogs' Home, as Gran once said). Mum thought that having two close together would make growing up more harmonious. (Fresh fuel for Rosie: 'You didn't *want* to have me! I was a mistake!' To which the obvious answer was, 'You are so right.') I suppose it did reduce stress while we were little. I could hardly remember having been an only child so we got on fine and only came close to killing each other about twice a month, and as we got older we drifted apart quite amicably, having different friends, doing different things.

So when we got back from the Harkers I was glad that Dad was with me. I'd forgotten that Jamze was home alone until we turned the corner and could feel the thumping from Jamze's music centre as well as hear it. His attic room is at the front and the window was open.

'How many times . . .?' Dad muttered. The people next door were tolerant and didn't use their attic anyway, but there are limits.

A head had appeared at the window in a halo of smoke. I didn't see if it was Jamze but if it wasn't, whoever it was spotted us for the thumping stopped dead. As we went up the steps and Dad was getting his key out, the front door was opened from the other side and four lads shot out, all in hoodies, with the hoods up, so that none of them seemed to have any shoulders. Two of them muttered, ' 'Evening, Mr Winchester,' as they poured down the steps in a fragrant cloud, heads hidden in hoods. The last one said, 'Hi, Clay,' but I couldn't tell who it was.

'Now what's the stupid prat been up to?' Dad said, still fumbling for his keys as the last of the hoodies had considerately closed the front door behind him.

'He thought you'd be out all evening,' I said.

The fragrance still lingered on the evening air. Dad sniffed as we went in.

'What are they smoking, for God's sake? Camel dung cut with Fairy Liquid?'

He stood at the foot of the stairs, looking fed up.

'Now I'll have to go and chew his ear. God, I can't leave him alone for five minutes.'

'It's more like three hours,' I said, 'and he wasn't expecting you back for ages. What did you think he'd do?'

'He never seems to do anything,' Dad said. 'Shall I ground him?'

'Would he notice?'

'I'm not having that stuff in here whatever it is. It's bad enough with Marina . . .'

He was on the way upstairs, reluctantly.

'Don't you ever smoke it?' I said. '*Didn't* you?'

'Difficult to believe,' Dad said, 'but at his age I couldn't afford it. It was much harder to get hold of, anyway. Most people didn't even think about it. Ten Woodbines, that was my limit.'

'The print unions?'

'Ah, those dear dead names; SOGAT, NATSOPA . . . gone the way of NACODS. Just saying them aloud makes me feel old. What shall I do to him?'

'Give him hell.'

It wouldn't happen, of course. Dad didn't know how to give anyone hell. After he had ascended to the attic I went up to my room and I could hear voices – well, one voice, Dad's. I assumed that in the pauses

Jamze was grunting. After a bit there were footsteps on the stairs and Jamze went by looking sheepish, with an armful of cider cans. As depravity went, Jamze wasn't very good at it, frankly. A bit later Dad passed the door looking relieved.

That evening Dad and I – Jamze having declined to join us – went down to the studio to watch *McCabe and Mrs Miller* at my request.

'Any particular reason?' Dad said, fast-forwarding through *The Railway Children*.

'I've just thought, it's the only town in a Western with a hill in it.'

'Probably because it was shot on location. Most of the early ones would have been filmed on the studio back lot. There'd have been a permanent set; general purpose frontier high street.'

That's not the only difference, though. The movie begins in rain and ends in a snow storm with a gunfight between McCabe and the three heavies. And unlike *High Noon* the whole town isn't there to watch, concealed and fearful. The church has caught fire and they're all trying to put it out. No one even knows about the shoot-out, all four men are killed and the snow covers the corpses. Nobody will find them until the thaw, and even then they won't know what happened, or care. It's a miserable thought that you could die and no one would know, although unless there's an afterlife you wouldn't know that either. It must be even worse to be afraid that no one notices you are alive.

I thought Mum and Gran would come reeling home in the small hours but they were back by half past ten, just as the credits rolled. I saw the light go on in the living room and went to get the lowdown.

'It's not over already, is it?'

'Not exactly,' Mum said. She didn't look happy.

'*Dance of the Vampires. Night of the Living Dead,*' Gran said. 'It all got very murky.'

'That was probably when the sun went down,' I said. 'You had your garlic with you, didn't you?'

'I'm not in the mood,' Mum said, very snappy for her. 'I'm going to bed. Is Jamie back?'

'He never went away,' I said softly, but she'd already gone upstairs. 'What happened?' I asked Gran. 'Was there a row?'

'No.' Gran wasn't looking too cheery either. 'A row would have been all right, it might have cleared the air. A really good wing-ding with frangible missiles – ideal spectator sport. They could show it late night on Channel 4. No, this wasn't half so much fun, wasn't fun at all. About as entertaining as a grumbling appendix that won't burst. Did you notice anything, Clay?'

'Like what?' I said, carefully.

'Well, what's-his-face and her . . .'

'Sandor and Ali.'

'The same. They weren't even there when we arrived, were they? Sandor Mark II—'

'Oz.'

'Thank you. Oz was doing the honours. Then out *he* comes, tripping the light fantastic, glad-handing all round the garden, and then she turned up looking extremely peeved.'

More than peeved, I thought. I said, 'We left soon after.'

'Yes, well, you were well out of it. They didn't speak to each other the whole of the evening – and it wasn't just that they didn't speak to each other, she was avoiding him. You know, things ought to have been getting lively by then, not to say out of hand given the amount of booze on tap, but people were restrained . . . edgy.'

'Surprised you noticed,' I said.

'Don't be a shrew,' Gran said. 'This fiction you

have of an ageing hippy is all very amusing but the occasional joint and the odd night on the sauce hardly amounts to a life of sex, drugs and rock 'n' roll, does it? I'm a teacher, for crying out loud. I'm sixty-three and I'm still teaching. I haven't taken early retirement, I love my work, but Christ, if I can't kick over the traces now and again . . .'

She went upstairs, really angry. I stayed in the living room feeling terrible, wiped out. Gran, my lovely Gran, angry with *me*.

But I knew that she wasn't so much angry as upset and it hadn't been me who'd upset her.

Mum didn't come down again either.

I took Addington Road very slowly on Sunday morning, with number 107 in view all the way. Now I'd seen the layout I knew that the upstairs window to the right of the porch must be the one where I'd heard Ali crying, not that I had any hard evidence that it had been Ali. The curtains were drawn, as usual; they must still be in bed. I tried to imagine it, what it was like having to get into bed with someone you've just had an almighty row with, not a quick fiery bust-up but a dreadful drawn-out stand-off that's been going on all day. Maybe she'd made him sleep in another room, unless that's only something that happens on television. Mum and Dad didn't even have fiery bust-ups, probably because they don't see that much of each other during the day; anyway, you try not to think too much about your parents in bed together.

They'd been married for seventeen years and together for a couple of years before that, so they must have had *some* fiery bust-ups in the early days at least, but nothing that I could remember, nothing that had shaken anyone else's foundations. Before Daisy's parents split, she'd woken one night and heard crashes downstairs and gone to look in case it was a) a burglar or b) the cat trying to kill something large that had escaped, and found her mother throwing dining room chairs at her father, really throwing them, through the air, down the length of the table. They were the sort of people who had a real dining room and a special table and chairs to go in it, as the Harkers did. I'd somehow thought that people like that wouldn't chuck the furniture at each other, but if you're angry enough . . .

Jake Sorley's mum and stepdad hated each other so much they didn't just row in front of the kids, they did it in front of anyone who happened to be there. I remember once standing in their hall, waiting for

Jake to come down, and these two were screaming abuse from different rooms. Mrs Sorley came out of the kitchen and ran upstairs, still screaming, screaming as she passed me, calling her husband every filthy name, screaming as she passed Jake at the top. Jake's two half-sisters were looking through the banisters and crying. They were not screaming, not making any sound at all. We'd been going to go swimming, a whole bunch of us, but Jake went back up and fetched the girls and we took them to the cinema instead to see *Shrek*, and bought them popcorn and ice creams, but all they really wanted us to do was cuddle them. We had them on our laps by the middle of the film, one each. Georgia, the younger one, never stopped shaking.

At least Ali and Sandor hadn't been doing that. I supposed that they'd been trying to be civilized. Ali had tried to be civilized with Oz's help. Oz was chivalrous, funny word, but that's how I thought of him; knowing what was the right thing to do and doing it. Sandor, it seemed to me, had been doing all the wrong things, and not because he didn't know any better, almost as if he was *trying* to stir things up.

Like Rosie, choosing exactly the right moment to

throw her strop, when she had a full house. I don't count Jamze in the full house. Rosie could set fire to her hair and fling herself downstairs and Jamze would only grunt, even if he passed her on the way up. Sandor should try stirring things up for Jamze's benefit and see what sort of a reaction he got: zilch. It struck me then that Sandor didn't take much notice of men. He hadn't at his party – or at ours, come to think of it. In fact, at ours he had more or less behaved as if Dad and John Iverson weren't there.

Dad as usual was in the studio when I got back. He doesn't observe Sunday as a day of rest unless he's really got nothing to do and he was already at work. I leaned in at the window.

'Did you speak to Sandor on Saturday?' I said. 'Did he speak to you, I mean?'

Dad hardly looked up from the screen. 'It would be nice,' he said, quite levelly, 'if there were a conversation in this house that didn't mention Sandor Bloody Harker.'

'I haven't been talking about him,' I said. 'Anyway, it was you who said he'd murdered his wife.'

'A joke's a joke,' Dad said. 'Joke over.' He looked up. 'Sorry, love, that's not fair. But I've only met the bugger twice. I'm just tired of hearing his name.'

Which meant that Mum must have been talking about him last night. I wondered what Dad had said to *her*.

Rosie came back from her sleepover in top form, half-way through an argument before anyone else had opened their mouths.

Rosie: I'll be going to Emma's straight from school tomorrow. Right?

Mum: No, it's not all right. You're coming home first, just as you always do.

Rosie: Why should I always have to do what I always do just 'cos I always do it? I've made arrangements.

Mum: Well, you'll have to unmake them, won't you? Get your thumbs out.

Rosie: Why are you always going on about my thumbs?

Mum: Most of the time it's the only part of you that moves.

Gran: Research has shown that the present generation is growing up with over-developed thumbs, through excessive texting. Next thing we know you'll have RSI and spend your adult life with two grotesquely enlarged *rigid digits*. Texter's syndrome. (Gran, by the sound of it, is also back on form)

Rosie: Just because you can't work a mobile . . .

Gran: Oh yes I can. I spend much of my time confiscating the sodding things. No texting allowed in modern languages. They can do it in art.

Mum: Go and let Emma know you'll be coming home first.

Rosie: You just want to ruin everything all the time, that's the only pleasure you get, ruining things for other people.

Mum: That's right. I lie awake at night planning how to wreck your life. Don't deny it – I won't be happy till you're dead.

Rosie: I don't know why you ever had me. I didn't ask to be born.

Gran: Well, next time you don't want to be born let us know in advance, will you? It will save a lot of bother. If you were going to ride roughshod over her wishes, Anna, you should have had her twenty years ago. She'd be out of our hair by now.

(Door slams)

I thought of that door slamming upstairs as Dad and I were leaving the party. Ali or Sandor? We'd all grown out of door-slamming except for Rosie, who was just growing into it. Jamze never slammed doors. It would use up too much valuable energy and in any case it would show that he *cared*, a dangerous weakness.

I didn't stay in the kitchen, I went straight upstairs, got out my school stuff and sat down to work. Gran and Mum were getting the lunch started, they'd be talking and I could guess what they would be talking about. I really didn't want to be stuck in any conversation about Sandor and Ali. I hadn't thought about it until Dad said what he had. We'd got our party postmortem out of the way before we'd reached home.

Why did the Harkers matter so much? We hardly knew them.

Four

Penny Iverson's craft shop is in Michelhampton, one of those villages on the river that fill up at weekends with people who like the idea of messing about in boats without actually having to do it. That means sitting at tables outside the three riverside pubs watching people who do have boats messing about in them. When they come out of the beer garden at the Heron, feeling at peace with the world and not too worried about money, there on the other side of the road is Stitchwort, Penny's shop, waiting to lure them in and sell them things they don't need. Originally the shop stocked wool and knitting patterns and needlework goods, hence the name, but when Penny took over she didn't want to change it and quite a lot of what she sells contains natural fibres.

Everything is hand-made and most of it makes you realize that mass production isn't all a bad thing: hand-made greetings cards, hand-dyed scarves, the sort of pottery Gran stopped making forty years ago, wind chimes and crystals and metalwork – candlesticks that are wiry and twisted as if they had been gripped and wrenched out of shape by some mad scientist after he has drunk the potion. To go in them are hand-dipped candles, hanging in bunches from hooks in the low beam that runs across the shop which also looks hand-made, like you do in Year One when you are learning about buildings. It is the third in a row of cottages with sway-backed roofs and tiny bow windows in their whitewashed walls. Everything is on the slant due to subsidence, but it is *ancient* subsidence so it just looks quaint instead of a poor insurance risk.

People who go in there must imagine that in the other picturesque cottages that line Michelhampton High Street are village housewives turning out Penny's stock behind their gingham curtains. Little do they know that the quaint cottages are empty all week because the people who own them live in London and the only activity behind the gingham curtains is burglars nipping in and out while the coast is clear. There are Neighbourhood Watch stickers everywhere, but no neighbours. Penny reckons she calls the police about twice a week on average. They rarely get there in time. Weekdays the air is filled with birdsong and the sound of alarms going off.

I wouldn't go near Michelhampton myself because it is like *The Village of the Damned* in reverse; instead of scary stary children there doesn't seem to be anyone under forty in the whole place, but towards the end of the summer term Penny offered me hard cash to go over one weekend and help her stocktake before the summer rush began.

The summer rush is only a rush compared to the winter trickle, but it gave Penny an excuse to clear out all the stuff which was entirely unsaleable and return it to its hopeful, hopeless craftspeople, to make room for things that even sober customers might want to buy. Everything there was on a sale or return basis; Penny never refused to display anything but she never promised to be able to flog it, either, and twice a year, the other time being after Christmas, she had a grand clear out. That was the stocktaking.

'They do take it,' she said grimly. 'They take it away.'

I cycled over. It had been dry for weeks, the lanes were dusty and although it was hot there was quite a wind. I fancied tumbleweeds rolling past my wheels, the distant hills were alive with the sound of war drums and the little white clouds above them were smoke signals. Here comes Clay Winchester, slouching low in the saddle, darting alert glances right and left from under the brim of her stetson, fingers resting lightly on the butts of them pearl-handled Colts.

Its being Saturday the cottages were full of weekenders rather than burglars and the car parks of the three pubs were overflowing onto the verges. There were vehicles down both sides of the High Street and a bus was trying to get through, while a tanker that had taken a wrong turning was backing up in a cloud of fumes. Something similar was happening on the river, just below the lock, where a pleasure craft loaded to the gunwales, a rented narrow boat and half a dozen cruisers were tangled up where the narrow boat had tried to do a U-turn. All you could hear on the road, on the river, were churning engines and angry voices, and outside the pubs were all those idiots kidding themselves that they were in the heart of rural England. Soon they would be over at Stitchwort looking at genuine rural crafts, or they would have been only Penny had a notice on the door: 'Closed for Stocktaking'.

I went along the lane at the back, past the wheelie bins, and put the bike in the passage at the side of the shop. The rural English burglars out here have bolt cutters. Shackle locks and chains don't stand a chance.

I thought she'd hear me and come out to check that I wasn't one of the burglars. A little kitchen opens off the passage and the shop is reached through that. When I went into the kitchen I could hear voices in the shop although the connecting door was closed. There's a window in the door with a net curtain stretched over it so that if you're in the kitchen you can keep an eye on the customers although, as Penny admits, the kind of things she sells don't attract shoplifters. Through it I could see Penny talking to a man.

I assumed it was John although he seemed too tall and then I knew who it was by the voice. It was saying, 'There must be *something* here. I was pinning my hopes on you.'

It was Sandor Harker.

I wasn't particularly pleased, but after all, it was a shop, he had as much right to be there as anyone else. Then I remembered that Penny had the 'Closed' sign on the door. I didn't hear what she said but Sandor carried on.

'You mean there isn't one single thing here that I can persuade you to sell me?'

There was that whimsical, challenging note in his voice as if he was trying to entice her into using her feminine wiles to sell him something he didn't want; almost flirty. I'd never seen Penny flirt, well, she'd always been with John. After twenty years they must have got past flirting – with one another.

'Ali's very fussy about what she wears,' Penny said. 'What makes you think she'd want any of this ... tat?' Through the curtain I saw her arm go out in a sweeping gesture towards the clothes rack where she keeps ethnic-type skirts and tunics and trousers made in India by women who would never wear things like that themselves. I certainly couldn't imagine Ali wearing them.

There was something in Penny's tone that gave me the impression that she was trying to get rid of him. To give her a helping hand I jerked the door open. 'Hi!' I said, loud and bright, not surprised to see him or anything, just barging in, the way I usually do.

And Sandor did what I'd seen him do before, spring away from Penny although, as before, he hadn't been doing anything to spring away from.

'Where did you come from?' he said, as though I'd snuck up on them.

'There's a back way in,' I said. 'I thought the shop was shut.'

'Oh!' That wicked conspiratorial glance again. 'Then I'll slip out that way.'

'No need,' Penny said, irritably, and made to unbolt the shop door, but Sandor was already shimmying past me into the kitchen.

'This way?'

'Don't fall over my bike,' I said.

Sandor put a finger to his lips and ogled Penny. 'Not a word to Ali, remember. This is meant to be a surprise.' Then he was out in the passage, still making faces through the closing gap as he shut the door. We watched him pass the kitchen window, find his way blocked by wheelie bins, turn round and go back in the other direction.

I was just going to say, 'What was all that about, then?' when Penny said, 'What was all that about?'

'I don't know,' I said. 'I missed the first reel.'

'I was sorting scarves when I saw a shadow on the wall and there he was at the window, making hand signals.'

'What, slowing down, please overtake?'

'No, pointing to the door and miming, "Let me in".

So I did. If I'd left him out on the street he might have got arrested for performing without a licence.'

'What did he want?'

'I think he's mad,' Penny said, as if she meant it. 'He said he was just passing when he remembered that this was my shop and he was sure I'd have something he could get Ali for her birthday.'

'Had he forgotten it, then? Anyway, this isn't the sort of place, I mean . . .'

'Don't let's fool ourselves,' Penny said. 'This may be my shop but I don't pretend to be selling great art. God knows what made him think there'd be anything here that Ali would want. You've seen her. Whistles and Agnés B, not Stitchwort. Anyway, it's half one on a Saturday afternoon. All he needs to do is drive into town and find her a proper present.'

'Perhaps he wanted something . . . different?' I suggested.

'What, like this?' Penny picked up a doorstop made of a house brick covered in patchwork. 'Or this?' One of the candlesticks, apparently plaited out of barbed wire. 'This?' A perfectly good silk scarf ruined with hand-painted ivy leaves that looked like dinosaur footprints. 'Do me a favour.'

'Why didn't he want you to tell Ali? He didn't buy anything anyway.'

'What did he think I was going to do, ring her up specially and grass on him? I haven't seen her in weeks.'

'Since the party?'

'Oh no,' Penny said, 'they've been round a couple of times since then and we went for a drink with them – ran into them at a concert. I can't say Ali ever seems very keen . . . anyway, let's get on. All that stuff on the side table's got to be packed. Wrap them up and put them back in the right boxes. Makers' names are on the labels – you know the drill. I'll make us some coffee, OK?'

'Cool.'

Penny doesn't hang about. She took over Stitchwort because she couldn't bear not having something to do when she was made redundant and she liked the idea of running a shop, but she didn't realize what she'd end up selling. Unfortunately, all her craft ladies love her so much she hasn't the heart to change to selling something different. She once told Mum that it might be as fulfilling to work on the checkout in Tesco. At least food serves some useful purpose in life, unlike the artefact I was just then packing, a papier mâché mask polished with bronze powder; West African, or West Bucks.

Penny had nipped to the loo while the kettle boiled so she was out of earshot when someone rapped on the window. The sun was behind them, all I could see was that it was a woman peering in. I smiled pleasantly and pointed to the door where the sign said 'Closed for Stocktaking' in very large letters, but she rapped again and pointed to the door herself. 'Let me in.'

This was just what Penny had said Sandor had been doing and then I saw that the woman was Ali. That's a coincidence, I thought and then, simultaneously, Bugger – he didn't want her to know he'd been here. I leaned towards the window over a display of collectible teddy bears and mouthed, 'Just a minute,' still smiling. She wasn't smiling back, there was something tense and grim about her, and unkempt, which was why I hadn't known her at first because when I thought of her, which was not all that often, I pictured her as she had been that afternoon when she came round with the flowers, when I opened the door and found her on the step. She rapped on the glass again, hard.

I called out loud, 'Just a minute!' and went to the

kitchen door, just as Penny came back. 'Guess who's making hand signals now,' I said. 'Ali Harker's trying to get in.'

'*What?*' Penny must be having the same thought that I'd had. 'Damn, that couldn't be worse timing. Finish off the coffee – only needs pouring.'

I poured, so I didn't witness Penny clambering through the papers and boxes in the shop but I heard her unbolting the door and starting to say, I suppose, 'Ali! What a surprise.'

And I heard Ali *crash* in. 'Where is he?'

She didn't say it, she shouted. I had that feeling again I'd had at the party, Something's going on, I don't want to know – stay out of it – let the grown-ups sort it out. But I couldn't leave Penny to do the sorting. I picked up the mugs and went through to the shop.

Penny was shutting the door again, before anyone else tried to follow. 'Where's who? There's only me and Clay Winchester here.'

'I saw him come in,' Ali said. 'Where is he? He didn't come out.'

'There's a back way,' I said, 'past the bins.' Ali shoved me aside, slopping the coffee, crossed the kitchen and looked into the passage. 'What's upstairs? Where are the stairs?'

'It's a flat,' Penny said. 'Nothing to do with the shop. It's got a separate front door. Ali, do stop, calm down; look, come and sit here, have some coffee; Clay, make another cup. How do you like it, I forget.'

She was gabbling, sounding guilty. What was there to sound guilty about?

'He left when I came,' I said, and realized as I said it that this wasn't going to help matters.

'Oh, I *bet* he did,' Ali said. She was shaking. 'When did you get here?'

'Ages ago,' I said. In fact it was hardly ten minutes but I didn't mean to lie. Ages ago – it's just something you say. 'I came in the back way too.'

Penny was still trying to act as if there had been a little misunderstanding, those mythical crossed wires again. 'You've only just missed him. Were you supposed to be meeting him? He can't have gone far – has he got his mobile? Call him.'

'Meeting him? *Here?*' Ali was grinding her teeth. 'Oh no. I wasn't supposed to know he was here, was I?' She shoved back into the shop as though she thought Sandor might be hiding somewhere.

Penny saw a straw and clutched at it. 'No, you weren't, actually. He was looking – he swore us to secrecy – he wanted to get you a birthday present.'

Ali started to laugh, a horrible false barking. 'A present? For me? This crap?' She grabbed a fistful of ethnic garments and ripped them off the hangers. The hangers were plastic, two of them snapped and one spun round the rail on its hook and took off across the shop, hitting a wind chime on the way that bucked and clashed. Ali flung down the clothes and snatched up a candlestick. 'This?' She slung it towards the window but the collectible teddy bears cushioned the impact. 'This?' The wind chime was still jangling. She tore it down and threw it after the candlestick but it was too lightweight to do any damage.

'Ali, stop it, you'll hurt yourself.'

I didn't think Penny was in the least bothered about Ali hurting herself, it was the stock she was worried about, and the mirror-backed shelves, and the window. Anyway, Ali didn't stop. She scythed her arm across the table where I'd been packing and sent everything flying, and screamed, 'You lying bitch! Where are the stairs? How do I get upstairs?'

Her hand came out like a claw, aiming for Penny's face, but Penny saw it coming and got one in first. She gave Ali such a slap that she staggered and nearly fell over. I was still standing in the doorway, clutching the coffees. I couldn't move, I was frightened; I thought they were going to start fighting and I didn't want to be there. It wasn't like school where everyone would be yelling 'Fight! Fight! Fight!' or on telly where it was supposed to be funny, or erotic, two women scrapping. But before I could even begin wondering what to do Penny grabbed Ali and put her arms round her and Ali buried her face against her shoulder and started to cry, loud and angry, like Rosie, but not like Rosie because this was real, out of control.

Penny was in control, though. She was like a mother comforting some kid who's gone OTT. I slithered back into the kitchen and made the third coffee, hearing Ali sobbing on the far side of the door, left theirs on the working surface and took mine out the back. I leaned moodily on a wheelie bin like Humphrey Bogart on the bar in *Casablanca*, and wished I was a smoker because I thought, If I was, now would be the time for it.

After a bit Penny came out and said, 'I'm going to drive Ali home. Will you be all right, cycling?' She could see I was shaken.

'I'll stay here and clear up,' I said. 'You won't want to come back to . . . all that.' I thought of the wreckage Ali had left.

'No, I'll see to it tomorrow. I need several stiff drinks now.'

'Shall I come back tomorrow?'

'If you can face it,' Penny said. She's about Mum's age and looks much younger, probably on account of not having had children, but she looked old now, shocked. 'Do you know, she's been sitting over there in her car outside the Heron, watching this place. God knows what ideas she's got in her head.'

'What about hers?'

'Her what – ideas?'

'Her car. If you're taking yours—'

'I really do not care,' Penny said. 'They can sort it out between them. You know, she followed him here.'

'Why? Did she know he was coming to see you?'

'He wasn't coming to see me,' Penny said. 'I haven't a clue where he was going. I think he knew she was after him. You get off home now, I'll pick you up about two, tomorrow, if you're still up for it.'

'I'd rather cycle,' I said. 'I like it.'

She turned to go back in and then said, 'What are you going to tell Anna?'

I hadn't thought that far ahead. 'I don't tell Mum everything.'

'Well, if you do, let me know, will you? Otherwise I'll keep quiet about it too. Poor Ali. I'm sorry, Clay, this is none of your business.'

'It's none of yours either, is it?' I said.

She said 'No,' and it was only then that I wondered if perhaps it might have been. Penny had said Sandor had only been there a few minutes but Ali knew it had been half an hour. A few minutes . . . ages ago . . . just something you say . . . isn't it?

I kept thinking about that as I cycled home. I crossed the river at the lock and went the long way round because I didn't want to be overtaken on the main road by Penny and Ali in the car. Why did Penny not want to talk to Mum about it? They'd been friends for so long, I'd have thought it was exactly the kind of thing they'd want to talk about.

I wanted to talk about it but I didn't know who to tell. Dad had made it clear that he was tired of hearing Sandor's name. That had been a long while back but I didn't imagine that he'd changed his mind. Gran? She'd be sympathetic but she'd wonder why I hadn't told Mum. Penny hadn't exactly *asked* me not to – she might do it herself, even though she'd said she wouldn't unless I did. Then Mum would wonder why I hadn't said anything.

Was Penny trying to protect Ali who'd kicked up such a stink about nothing and made herself look stupid and hysterical – or trying to protect herself because it hadn't been about nothing and she really was seeing Sandor in secret?

Surely she couldn't be seeing Sandor in secret. Anyway, she had been expecting me to turn up at one thirty even if she hadn't been expecting him . . . I got off the bike and sat down on the verge and texted Daisy: Nd 2 tlk.

I didn't want to talk to Daisy about what had happened at Stitchwort, I wanted to talk to someone about something before I went home and couldn't talk to anyone about anything.

Why mustn't I say anything?

Daisy didn't answer at once. I sat on the verge and waited. It is properly rural there, the cow parsley was high although if I focused I could see the traffic on the ring road through it, but it was a long way off, the traffic noises just a distant roar. There was a housing estate only two fields away but it felt peaceful, not like the scrum around Michelhampton.

I was annoyed when I heard a car coming.

The lane is straight there and so narrow that grass grows down the middle of it. The car was approaching quite slowly and when it came close it got even slower. I saw there was a man driving and thought a) he's going to ask directions to somewhere I've never heard of or somewhere I have heard of but don't know how to get to and he'll think I'm an airhead and b) he's going to try and abduct me; and I had a horrible preview of my abandoned bike lying by the roadside and police cars and a taped-off area. And bunches of flowers withering in a little shrine for months afterwards, left by my friends.

Mainly I just thought, Oh shit, I can't be bothered. Before the car had stopped I'd stood up so that if he was a would-be rapist he could see that it might not even be worth the effort, and turned the bike round so that if he tried *anything at all* I'd have a head start. There was no room there to turn a car, even a Mini, and this was an Audi, left-hand drive, so the driver was on my side of the road when he stopped and I'd already recognized him. It was Sandor. I'd forgotten that he was still at large.

'Had an accident?' he said, as though nothing else had happened – well, he didn't know it had.

'No. I'm just texting a friend.'

'Texts are a whole new language,' he said, as though he had come up with this idea himself. 'It's as impenetrable as Japanese. I'll have to get you to show me how, sometime.' Then he dropped the charming ignorance, and frowned.

'I thought you were at the shop with Mrs Iverson.'

'She had to go home . . . for something.'

'Can I give you a lift anywhere? Put the bike on the rack.'

Never get into cars with strange men. And he was quite strange enough to be going on with.

'No, thanks, I'm just going for a ride.' Of course, now the bike was facing in the direction we'd both come from.

He started to draw in his head, then said, 'You didn't see Ali while you were in Michelhampton, did you?'

'No, why, was she there too?'

That floored him. 'Oh, I just thought she might have been . . .'

I wanted to ask him why he thought that, but I didn't really want to hear whatever reason he gave because it wouldn't be the real one. I just wanted him to go away but he sat there at the wheel, frowning.

'See you, then,' I said breezily and swung into the saddle, ready to ride off into the sunset down the Old Chisholm Trail. I waved, without looking round, and I didn't look round when I heard him drive off. I kept pedalling until I was sure the Audi was out of sight. Now I was going the wrong way, back to Michelhampton where I did not want to be, so as soon as I knew I had the road to myself, I turned round again.

What was he playing at? Had he *known* that Ali was somewhere around when he went into the shop, had he suspected that she was watching for him. Penny had said something about that. Why had she been watching for him . . .?

I'd hardly gone two hundred metres when I looked up and saw the Audi ahead, coming back again. He must have turned as soon as the lane became wide enough. If I could see him he could see me, but I didn't care, I didn't want any more conversations where I hadn't had time to read the script or even find out what the plot was. I was just coming to a little wooded area without any fencing. There was a ditch alongside the verge but I was off the bike and over it in seconds, and by the time the Audi went past I was out of sight among the brambles.

I heard it slow down though, and for a horrible moment I thought he was going to stop and come looking for me – he must have seen me swerving off the roadway, even from a distance, although he wouldn't have known exactly where. I didn't have assault on my mind, that wasn't what I was hiding from, but I couldn't face talking to him. This was what Rosie and her friends were evading when they walked the streets stony-faced, never making eye contact with anyone. Gran used to joke, 'It's a well-known fact that if you allow an *old* person, that is, anyone over the age of eighteen, to look into your eyes they will steal your soul.' I used to think she was on to something, having been blanked frequently in public by my own sister, but now I knew what Rosie was afraid of. How do you respond to people when you don't know how their minds work?

When the sound of the engine had died away completely I went back to the road and pedalled like fury until I came to a turning, desperate to be out of sight in case he came back *again*. In the end I made so many detours it took me an hour to get home instead of twenty minutes and it wasn't fun. It would have been once, dodging and weaving to throw an enemy off the scent; I'd have pretended I was Butch Cassidy and the Sundance Kid on the run from the men who are tracking them with uncanny persistence across country, never seen in close up, never more than a faraway cloud of dust by day, a little cluster of lights at night, never wavering, never slackening, always coming onwards, until they are so close that Butch and Sundance leap off a high rock into a fast-running river to escape them.

They were fleeing for their lives; I wasn't that desperate and I don't think I'd have jumped into a river to escape, even a river like ours which is old and slow and only a metre down from the bank. But I was angry and miserable because I still couldn't figure what was going on between Sandor and Ali.

Only it wasn't just between Sandor and Ali, that was the trouble. If it had been I would have said something to Mum. I ought to have done. It wasn't long before I wished I had.

If I'd been asked, then, 'Daisy's your best friend, isn't she? Do you tell her everything?' I'd have said yes, although Daisy always had told me a lot more than I'd told her, mainly because she had so much more to tell.

One thing she told me often was, 'Ohmygod, you're so *lucky*.' She didn't mean everyday luck, like finding a tenner outside WH Smith (she was the one who did that) or getting fabulous presents and hunky boyfriends – Daisy again. She meant my family. Her own was such a mess that she really envied mine, parents who were obviously going to stay married for ever and ever, laid-back granny, and all of us getting on so well and enjoying each other's company. Discounting Rosie and Jamze she was right and even they would come in from the cold eventually. In spite of the sulks and strops Rosie knew that she was safe and loved (she would never have risked making herself so deeply unlovable otherwise) and although I sometimes wondered if Jamze had any sensory perceptions at all, he would have felt it soon enough if that safety net had been taken away. So I heard a lot more about Daisy's troubles than she did about mine, but when she finally got back to me I was at home.

'What do you need to talk about?'

I realized that I didn't want to talk about it any more because I didn't know what to say without making it sound entertaining, and it hadn't been entertaining. I invented something about homework and she said, 'Will you come to me or me to you?'

'You come here.'

Everyone was out except Dad in the studio, and he had some deadline coming up so I was leaving him alone. Daze came over and we sat in the garden up by the back door in the sun and did the work which in fact I wasn't having any trouble with. I ended up helping her.

'Weren't you supposed to be working at that shop today?' she said. 'Isn't that why you didn't come down town with us?'

'We switched it to tomorrow,' I said, which was the truth, and I was just about to add, 'Daze, something really weird happened,' when she went on, 'You don't mind being with old people all the time, do you?'

'It's not all the time,' I said, 'and they're still people, even if they're old. Anyway, they're not all that old.'

'Your gran, your dad, that clockwork woman—'

'Stitchwort. She's only Mum's age.'

'How old's your mum, then?'

'Forty-two.'

'It's not really *young*, is it? What do you talk about?'

I thought about it and the truth was, I didn't talk all that much to Mum, not as much as I did to Gran and Dad. Age matters a lot when there's only a little gap – think how you despise the infants when you get to Year Three – but the bigger it gets the less you notice it; like an elephant and a poodle. The elephant takes up much more room but it just stands there and after a bit you stop noticing it, but the poodle goes on yapping and jumping about. Perhaps that's what Daze meant. She gave me one of her little lectures about how I wouldn't learn anything about men from Dad and I thought of telling her what I'd learned from another man I'd been observing lately, but at that stage I wasn't sure what I was learning.

Still, when Mum came home from work a couple of weeks later and found me in the kitchen and said quietly, 'Have you got a moment, Clay?' I remember thinking, This doesn't happen often. What have I done?

Jamze was out and Rosie was in the garden and there was no one else around on the ground floor, but she beckoned me into the back living room.

'Why didn't you tell me about Ali Harker and Penny?' she said. 'At the shop, that time.'

For a moment I couldn't remember why. Then I did remember and I felt my face going red. But I couldn't say, 'I don't think Penny wanted me to.'

'I forgot,' I said.

'Forgot? How could you forget? It must have been ghastly. I can't think why Penny didn't say anything.'

'Who told you, then?' I said, seeing that there were only two people it could have been, if Penny hadn't.

'Sandor did,' Mum said, and for the first time I really didn't like hearing her use his name. 'He's in rather a state—'

'*He's* in a state?' I said, remembering Ali trying to smash up the shop.

'Upset,' Mum corrected herself. 'Ali's having emotional problems . . .' Translation: she's nuts, I thought to myself. '. . . she's been pretty irrational lately and he can't get her to seek help . . .'

'I wasn't there for long,' I said, 'at the shop, I mean. What happened? What does he say happened?'

'It all got out of control – simple misunderstanding,' Mum said. 'He was passing through Michelhampton and he thought he'd drop in on Penny to see if there was anything he could get Ali for her birthday.'

Mum, unlike me and Penny – and Ali – didn't see anything improbable in that.

'And apparently Ali had been following him.'

'On foot?'

'Oh, don't be silly, she's got a VW. Just after he'd gone she burst in on Penny and more or less accused her of having a clandestine relationship. Well, you were there, weren't you?'

'She was upset . . .' I was thinking, Why has he told her this? 'But I went out the back. I didn't want to listen.'

'You didn't hear what got said, then.'

'No.' First I hadn't told her and now I was lying to her. And I was trying to work out who knew what. If Ali had told Sandor, she'd have mentioned my being there, wouldn't she? But it sounded as though he hadn't known, so it must have been Penny and she'd been trying to keep me out of it. But he knew I'd been there; we'd spoken, and he hadn't tried to keep me out of it. I remembered our meeting on the road home when I'd told him I hadn't seen Ali. Was he trying to find out what I knew, in a roundabout way? I still wasn't any clearer but while I'd been going over it Mum must have said something else and was waiting for an answer.

'Well?' she said.

'Sorry?'

'How long was he there?'

'Where?'

'It's like talking to a wall . . . How long was Sandor at the shop?'

'He was there when I arrived – he was just leaving. Ali said he'd been there half an hour.'

'So you did hear—'

'Only that—'

'So you were out at the back and you didn't hear a thing? From what I can gather she was screaming and throwing things. *Why* didn't you—?'

I don't know how I was looking. I don't practise agonized expressions the way Rosie does – I caught her at it once in the bathroom mirror – but perhaps it was as miserable as I felt because Mum broke off quite suddenly and said, 'Darling, I'm sorry, it must have been hateful. No wonder you didn't want to talk about it. But don't bottle things up. Or did you say something to—'

'Gran or Dad? No. I didn't think they'd want to know.'

Mum sighed, as if she'd discovered that for herself, and I wondered what had made Sandor think that *she* would want to know. And now Mum must be asking herself why Penny hadn't said anything.

Include me out, I said to myself, in the immortal words of Sam Goldwyn, the great Hollywood producer.

What Mum also didn't know was that I never did go back to the shop the next day. Penny rang me on my mobile, not the house phone, and said not to bother, but she'd pay me anyway. And she did, she sent a cheque by post, for much more than she'd promised me, even though I'd hardly done anything. I could understand that she didn't want to talk about it either, not so soon after, but when that cheque came I felt as though I was being bought off.

Five

Apart from Dad's design award none of us ever wins anything – quizzes, raffles, competitions, guessing the number of marbles in a jar – so when Mum landed two theatre tickets in a draw at work she and Dad decided to make a night of it and went up to London for a meal before the show, and Gran cooked for us.

Jamze would happily live off pork scratchings but eats anything that is put under his nose. Rosie had been experimenting with allergies but that cut no ice with Gran:

Gran: If you die I'll happily accept the blame but I want to see you in your coffin first. Anyway, no one's allergic to pasta.

Rosie: It's got gluten in it.

Gran: I know it has. If you had a gluten aversion you wouldn't be able to eat pizza. You ought to do your research more thoroughly.

Rosie: I've got this rash—

Gran: Probably your stick-on tatoos. I'm making spaghetti blog and you are eating it. There's nothing else.

Rosie: There's stacks of stuff in the freezer—

Gran: Lay one finger on the freezer and I'll have it off. You've heard of a finger buffet, haven't you?

Rosie could have gone on hunger strike of course and come out with some rubbish about being in control of her body, but she was too fond of eating. Anyway, she liked real food, she just couldn't bear to accept anything without an argument in case the rest of us started taking her for granted.

Rosie: As soon as I'm old enough I'm going to leave home.

Gran: I doubt it.

Rosie: You can't stop me.

Gran: I wouldn't dream of trying.

Rosie: If I go to uni . . . (This is the first we've heard of uni. So far Rosie's plans have only included becoming famous)

Gran: If you go to uni you'll be home with your

dirty washing once a fortnight. After I left home I never went back. When Anna graduated she was back for three months till she found a job. Times have changed, my little pyroclastic cloud. When you've finished uni you'll be back here, probably for the rest of your life, you and your brother.

Rosie: You don't care what happens to me! (Heads for staircase, tear ducts ticking over)

Gran: Right now, no. Just so long as you're back here in twenty minutes; I'll be putting the pasta on at ten past.

And she was back, naturally. The sauce smelled too good to ignore and I'd made garlic bread which Rosie could never resist in spite of all the gluten. She told me much later that she'd got gluten mixed up with gluttony and she thought it was something that made you fat.

It was the start of the holidays for us. Gran had broken up a week earlier because St Catherine's is independent; longer hours, shorter terms. It had been warm and sunny all day, we had been going to eat on the paved bit outside the French windows but it started to cloud over around six and by the time Gran put the water on to boil for the spaghetti it was raining hard. Jamze, who knows what to do when this sort of thing happens, left me to get the cutlery and plates in and chose a DVD to watch while we ate. He knew that if he didn't Rosie would want *EastEnders* which we sometimes watch for a laugh but which Rosie believes is true to life. She has to make do with the omnibus on Sundays because if anyone else is there while she watches they get an endless commentary on the plot so far and explanations about who is related to whom. 'They are all related to each other,' Gran said. 'True to life? If they were that inbred in real life they'd have pointed heads and gravel rash on their knuckles.'

Jamze's DVD was out-takes from a show so lame you'd never have thought they'd bothered to take anything out. If it had just been Gran and me we'd have talked to each other, no visuals, but there's something off-putting about trying to hold a conversation when two of the people present won't say anything. It's as if you're interrupting their deep and innermost thoughts, although I wasn't at all sure that either of them had any.

Jamze expressed something that might have been 'Thank you' and got up to leave while he was still chasing the last threads of spaghetti round his plate:

Gran: Your turn to wash up.

Jamze: What do you mean, my turn? (God – a whole sentence! With a verb!)

Gran: As you haven't done it for about three weeks it must be your turn.

Jamze: I gotta go *out*.

Gran: Of course you have, but wash up first, eh?

Jamze: (Forgetting to growl and squeaking instead) I gotta *meeet* someone.

Gran: Come on, angel-face, do it to please your old granny – or I'll break your legs.

'You and whose army?' Jamze said, but he grinned and collected the plates. In those days I used to wonder what we'd do without Gran who was never offended by Rosie and Jamze when they were piggish, because she really didn't care what anyone else thought, never took an insult personally and managed to keep things off boiling point. Jamze would have stood and argued with Mum for so long that he could have washed up, gone out and come home again.

He was bashing about in the kitchen when the doorbell rang. He bellowed, 'That'll be Chazza! I'll get it!' galumphed along the hall and opened the door with a glad cry: 'Howzit goin', mate?'

Then there was silence. Then Jamze poked his head in, croaked, 'It's that geezer again,' and went back to the kitchen.

'How many geezers do we know?' Gran wondered and went to find out and I followed her because I remembered Jamze's last encounter with Sandor and I had a nasty feeling.

I was right. Sandor stood in the porch looking dishevelled and very wet, as if he had been running through the rain. I heard him say, 'Is Ali here?'

'No,' Gran said. 'Is she supposed to be? Roger and Anna are out.'

This was well put, I thought, as if to say, 'You are Anna's friend and therefore her responsibility. Whatever you're up to it's got nothing to do with me.'

Rosie came up under my elbow, took one look, muttered, 'Oh, *him*,' and turned to go upstairs. I grabbed her.

'What do you mean, "Oh, him"? You've never met him . . . have you?'

But Rosie was out of reach and I couldn't call her back without shouting.

'You'd better come in,' Gran was saying. 'Do you want some coffee? We've just finished eating.'

I thought, If someone turned up on the doorstep

bleeding to death we'd offer them coffee before we even thought about a tourniquet. I was about to offer to make it, because Jamze would never be able to manage that and do the washing up at the same time and anyway, he always uses instant, but Sandor seemed to be moaning faintly and running his hands through his dramatically dripping hair and I got the impression that coffee was not required at that moment, although Gran would be wanting hers. I thought I'd give it ten minutes and then knock discreetly because Gran was taking him into the front room. I heard her pull the glass doors across as I went into the back room and turned the telly right down so that they wouldn't be interrupted. The doors keep out the draughts but not much sound.

So of course I could hear what was going on. The panes are fake bottle glass and all I could see were warped shapes, both on the sofa, one at each end. You keep it that way, Sunshine, I thought.

Gran: Shall I get you a towel?

Sandor: No, no. I'll dry off – must have been mad – rushing out like that – no coat—

Gran: (Cheerily) Yes. Did you remember your keys?

Sandor: I had them on me. Sometimes I feel . . . as if I

am going mad ... nothing seems to make sense ... one moment we're fine, talking normally ... then she flares up – shouting things – accusations—

Gran: Well, have you done anything to be accused of?

Sandor: (Offended, I should think, not being accustomed to Gran) How could I? She's so jealous, she imagines every woman I speak to—

Clay: (Aside) And you do speak to a lot of them.

Sandor: She's always measuring herself against other people, convincing herself that I do the same, that I find her unsatisfactory. I know how young she is, but that's not natural, is it? (Despairing cry) Most young women are so confident, they walk about like goddesses ...

Gran: That's teenagers, not women.

Clay: (To self) Do I walk about like a goddess?

Gran: Anyway, Ali's a lovely girl. If she's not feeling confident perhaps it's because she thinks you don't appreciate her?

Sandor: But I do! I can't believe how lucky I am to have her.

Gran: Do you pay her enough attention? I mean

(Tactful pause) you're obviously very outgoing . . . with everybody.

Clay: With women.

Sandor: But that's how I am. That's how I've always been. Can I help it?

Gran: Perhaps you can help showing it. What happened this time?

Sandor: I don't know. We were just about to start the meal, start preparing it—

Gran: Oh, do you cook together? That's nice.

Sandor: I cook. Ali's more of a microwaver.

Clay: *Bitch*. (What do you call a male bitch?)

Sandor: I was just suggesting we took a little more time over it and she flung the bowl on the floor and rushed out. It was Dartington glass – fragments everywhere.

Gran: And you rushed after her? Didn't you see where she went?

Sandor: (Voice trembling with suppressed emotion) I was stunned. I couldn't move at first – she threw the bowl at me!

Having seen Ali in action I could imagine that she had launched the bowl with considerable force. I remembered her shying the candlestick at the window in Stitchwort. Penny remarked afterwards that it was a good thing I'd already packed the patchwork brick door stop.

Gran: Well, where did you think she might have gone – oh. Of course, you thought she'd come here. Why was that?

Sandor: You were the nearest. And . . . after that time with Penny—

Gran: What time with Penny?

Sandor: Oh, Ali got some crazy idea—

Gran: That you and Penny . . . and she suspects the same thing about *Anna*?

Sandor: She thinks the same about all my friends.

Clay: All your *women* friends.

Gran: Well, she didn't come here. Is she rushing around in the rain without a coat too?

Sandor: No, she took her car. (L-o-o-ong pause)

Gran: Let me get this straight; she *drove* off and you *ran* after her?

Sandor: I was distracted – not thinking – I just ran out into the street, calling her name – never mind the keys – I'm not sure I even shut the door.

And Mum had told *me* not to be silly when I asked if Ali had followed Sandør to Michelhampton on foot. The neighbours must have been enjoying it, I thought, remembering *Rear Window* lady with the crystals opposite, and imagining them all settling down at their windows with drinks and salted almonds for the evening performance. Then it hit me; I was eavesdropping. At the back of my mind was the idea that the more I knew about what was going on the better, but we'd been brought up not to listen in to other people's conversations. Most people are, I imagine, although these days it can be difficult not to. I walked up the High Street once in front of a girl who was yelling into her phone about genital warts, all the way. This was something I didn't much want to hear about. Why don't you text? I thought. There is probably a dedicated symbol for genital warts. But if I'd said anything she'd have gone postal because I was listening to a private conversation.

I went out of the room, very quietly. Jamze had finished in the kitchen. There was more water lying about than there would have been if one of the rest of us had washed up but at least everything showed signs of having been in and out of detergent. I got out the cafetière, switched on the kettle and stood looking out of the window, thinking about what Rosie had said.

I didn't know that she'd ever met Sandor. She hadn't gone to the party and the two times he'd come to the house she'd been out. But those were the only two that I knew about. He might have come round at other times, he might be a regular visitor – but when would he fit it in? One of us would have noticed – he'd have seen to that. But there must have been occasions when everyone was out but Mum.

And Rosie, evidently.

Jamze still didn't know who he was.

He would never have come round to see Dad or Gran – would he?

Mum didn't have to tell us when she had visitors, and who they were and why they came and how long they stayed. But I didn't like the thought of him coming to see her and us not knowing.

I didn't think Ali would like it, either.

I made the coffee and laid out a tray for Gran and Sandor, then I poured myself a mug and took the tray along to the front room.

My house; my front room; my gran. Why shouldn't I just walk straight in? Rosie would.

But you are not Rosie, I told myself as I wobbled

along the hall with the tray, trying to stop the cafetière sliding off. You are big sensible Clay, tactful Clay; so I balanced on one foot, steadied the tray against my knee and knocked, and called out, 'I've made coffee. Can you open the door?'

There was another of those pauses. Then Gran said, 'Can you just leave it in the hall, Clay? Thanks.'

I could have pretended I hadn't heard and somehow got the door open and walked in to see what was going on. But I didn't want to know at that particular moment. I had a feeling that if I did butt in I'd find Sandor, springing away from Gran the way he'd sprung away from me, and Penny.

Gran?

And I didn't want to bring up the subject with Rosie and make her feel that I was probing, make her feel that there was anything to probe about. For all the lip gloss and nail polish and accessories, Rosie was still about four years old underneath or she'd have realized that icy silence was more effective than tantrums in this household. But presumably tantrums worked for her friends. In the event I didn't have to say anything myself.

After I'd left the coffee I took mine upstairs to get on with some reading ahead for next term. I reckoned that if I did a bit every day I'd be off to a flying start in September. After about twenty minutes Rosie appeared in the doorway.

'It's so not fair.'

Most people start a conversation with 'Hi' or 'Hullo'; not Rosie. This was her normal opening gambit.

Clay: I know. Life's a bitch, isn't it?

Rosie: I just wanted to watch *The Bill*, I always watch *The Bill*.

Clay: It'll be half over by now, won't it?

Rosie: Everyone else I know's got a television in their room. Dad's so mean like that. He's got his own in the studio.

Clay: (Who can't see where this is going) Well, go and watch *The Bill*, then. No one's stopping you.

Rosie: Gran did. I went down and it was already on with that thing of Jamie's so I took it out and switched over and Gran came through from the front and told me to turn it off and go away.

Clay: Gran told you to go away?

Rosie: She's like, Stay out of the way for a bit, will

you? I wasn't in her way so I'm like, I'm not in your way, and she lost her rag and told me to go somewhere else. I mean, I'd have gone out but then I'd have got into trouble because no one knew where I was, you know how Mum's like: Never go anywhere without telling me first, all the time . . .

Clay: Yes, but you didn't go out, did you, so you won't get into trouble. (Seizing opportunity) Why did Gran throw you out?

Rosie: She said she was talking. She's always talking.

Clay: I think she meant she was having a conversation, something important. She didn't want *The Bill* banging on in the background.

Rosie: It was only with *him*.

Clay: Who?

Rosie: That man Mum knows. You know, he came after dinner. Jamie let him in.

Actually, Jamze had not let him in, Jamze had left him on the step, as usual. Best place for him, I was beginning to think.

'Have you met him before?' I asked innocently.

Rosie had come right in by now and was sitting on my bed, examining her feet.

142

'Verrucas?' I said, when she didn't answer.

'That's gross.'

'True. If you've got them I don't want you walking over anything I've got to touch. I said, where did you meet him?'

'Who?'

'The bloke Gran's talking to – Sandor.'

'I dunno. I was out with Mum.'

Rosie is not seen in public with any of us if she can avoid it. We spoil the image, whatever it is, so this must have been a particular occasion, i.e., they were buying something. For Rosie.

'When was that?'

'I don't *know*,' Rosie said, furiously. If I didn't work fast I was going to lose her. 'It was my *shoes*. For my *birthday*. Right? Satisfied?'

I wasn't.

'You met him in the shoe shop?'

'*Naaaah*. She took me to Pizzacato and he was there.'

'You had lunch with him and you can't even remember his name?'

'Who cares what his name is? No, he was at the bar and he came and had coffee or something with us afterwards. I didn't like him. He's creepy.'

'What do you mean, creepy?'

'Oh, you know what people are like, trying to make you talk and using words they don't understand trying to be like they're *young*. I mean, he's *old*, innee? And that other time—'

'What other time?'

'He came here, didn't he? Talking to Mum and when she went to get something he's like, "You know, your mother's a really special person, don't you? You're just like her." I'm like, Yuck! Excuse me?'

I doubted very much if Rosie had said anything of the sort, it's what she and her friends tell each other they say.

'He did that here?'

'*Naaaah*. At Pizzacato, whatever. He came here to borrow something, or something.'

I said, 'Don't use my pen to clean your toenails.'

Rosie shrieked, 'I'm not! I'm drawing tattoos on my feet. God, you are so revolting!' And left; taking the pen.

Sandor must be even flakier than I'd thought if he'd imagined that he could charm Rosie. I'd meant to ask her if Ali had been at the pizza house too, but I didn't think she had. Rosie's birthday is 28 June, so it had been well after the party, but before the bust up in Penny's shop.

How often did Mum see him, apart from at work? Wasn't seeing him at work enough? I didn't suppose that she'd gone on a secret assignation to Pizzacato with Rosie in tow, Rosie being guaranteed to put a blight on any social occasion.

Or had Sandor known that they were going to be there, or had he seen them through that long plate glass window and followed them in, or had it been a real coincidence? The last, I told myself, but what was going on in the front room?

Rosie had left my door open and as I got up to shut it I heard Gran call up from the hall, 'I'm going out for ten minutes,' and the front door open and close. I shot along the landing to Mum and Dad's room and looked down out of the window. From that angle all I could see was our giant umbrella leaving the premises by the front gate with two pairs of feet under it. Out on the pavement I saw that it was Gran and Sandor walking very close together as people sharing an umbrella have to do, but as they crossed the road I also saw Sandor perform a complicated manoeuvre by which he gallantly took the umbrella from Gran and tucked her arm into his and walked on the outside of the pavement like a gentleman should.

I thought she'd shake him off, but she didn't. The

four-legged thing walked on up the street and turned the corner by the bookie's. I guessed it was heading for Addington Road.

Next thing, the phone rang. I knew that Rosie and Jamze wouldn't answer it because they assumed that anyone worth speaking to would be using their mobiles. I made a dive for the one by the bed, but just as my hand touched it I pulled back and let it do the seven rings until the BT electronic woman cut in.

I don't know what I was afraid of, I just had that bad feeling, so I waited a couple of minutes and then dialled 1571 to see if there was a message. It was John Iverson.

'Anna, can you give me a call when you get back?' He sounded urgent, but then he started umming and erring the way people do if they get a machine when they were expecting a person, and frankly, the chances of our house being completely empty any time after five pm were so remote he must have been sure that a human being, or even Jamze, would pick up. 'Um – have you seen – ah – if you're with Penny tell her – uh – oh, no – tell her to give me a call – no – shit – sorry, 'bye. I'll be here. 'Bye.'

He sounded as though something had upset him but he didn't want to leave a message that just anyone might hear. Was he going to sit and wait by the phone? I thought I'd better speak to him and rang back. The phone was picked up instantly, as if he *had* been sitting by it.

'Anna?'

'No, it's me, Clay. I just got your message. Sorry, couldn't get to the phone before it stopped ringing.'

'Is Anna there?'

'No, that's why I called. Mum and Dad are in London – the theatre. They won't be back till after twelve. Can I take a message?' Then I remembered *his* message. 'Penny's not here.'

'I didn't think she was.' He sounded confused. 'I just thought . . . She's supposed to be having dinner with a friend.'

Supposed? 'Has something happened?'

He was quiet for a moment, then he said, 'You know the Harkers, don't you?'

How had I known he was going to mention the Harkers? 'Yes, Sandor was here just now.'

'Sandor was with *you*?'

'With Gran. He's just gone home. He was looking for Ali.' As I said it I thought perhaps I oughtn't to be talking about what was happening, but John sounded so relieved.

'Ali was here, just now,' he said, 'looking for Penny. Is Gran – Marina – there?'

'No, she went back with Sandor. They should be at his in about five minutes, if you ring. They're walking.'

'Thanks. I'll do that.'

Relieved didn't begin to describe it. He hadn't said why Ali was looking for Penny but I could guess. She must have roared off in the VW after hurling the Dartington glass bowl at Sandor – and told John of her suspicions, which was why he had sounded so happy when I said Sandor was with Gran. Ali evidently hadn't bothered to mention that she'd left Sandor at Addington Road when she came out, and there was John, worrying that instead of having dinner with an old friend, Penny was doing the nasty with Sandor.

Had Penny told John what happened at Stitchwort? I didn't think she had, somehow. From what she'd said then, she and John knew the Harkers better than we did, but not much better, and yet everywhere we turned there was one Harker or another, turning up and causing trouble, as they were at that very moment, ricocheting all over the district like pinballs and cannoning into everyone but never, unfortunately, hitting each other.

That image made me start to smile but then I

thought, a) maybe he does hit her, and, b) what if she comes here next?

I couldn't face that, not with Gran out. The house was full of potential missiles. Suppose I couldn't get rid of her? I went up to Rosie's room and knocked. There was no answer. I opened the door and looked in. Rosie, with her tattooed feet, was lying on her bed, thumbs going like the clappers. When she heard me come in she bounced up in a rage.

'I'm *busy*. All right? If I don't say come in I *mean* don't come in, I don't want you in here, if I wanted you in here I'd ask you, innit? I don't come shoving into your room.'

'Yes you do,' I said. 'All the time, you did it just now. All I wanted to say was, if you hear the doorbell, don't answer it.'

Rosie's eyes became small and sly. 'Why not? You trying to avoid someone? I'll answer it if I want.'

I shouldn't have said anything. If I'd left her to her texting she'd have ignored the doorbell out of sheer bloody-mindedness.

'This isn't funny,' I said. 'I meant it. It may be someone none of us wants to see. I need to find out who's there before I open the door. All right?'

Rosie was just starting to slither off the bed, daring me to haul her back, although she knew I could, easily, when the doorbell rang. I don't think she'd been expecting it to happen so soon – neither had I – and she stopped in the middle of the slither long enough for me to get between her and the door and close it. She tried to push past but I wasn't having it.

'If I start screaming they'll know there's someone in.'

'If you start screaming I'll throw you on the bed and hold a pillow over your face.'

'You can kill someone like that.'

'That's the general idea.'

The bell rang again, a long angry burst, then a loud thumping at the knocker. Rosie stopped struggling and looked nervous.

'Who is it?'

'I don't know. I'm going down to see.'

'How—'

'Out of Mum's window.' It was risky. When people don't get an answer from a house that they know quite well is occupied, they stand back from the front door and glare up at the first floor windows to see if the upstairs curtains are twitching. I know, I've done it myself. But I was only half-way down the attic stairs when there came a really thunderous knocking on the back door.

'Don't go!' Rosie forgot about being Satan's spawn and clutched my arm. 'Clay, who is it?'

I was getting worried now. The knocking, bashing, came again as I reached the landing; then the phones started ringing.

One set in the hall, one in Mum and Dad's room, one in Gran's, coming up at us from all directions, three different ring-tones.

'Don't answer it,' Rosie begged. 'If it stops they'll know you're in.'

'It'll stop anyway,' I said, as the answering service took over.

There was a moment's silence and then my mobile began jingling in the bedroom. At the same time there were three crashing blows on the front door and what sounded like someone yelling through the letter box. Rosie collapsed on the stairs and started to cry. I wanted to join her. Why wasn't Jamze here? Even he would have responded by now. I wanted my mum.

But intrepid Clay Winchester shook off the clinging hands of Frenchie, queen of the saloon (*Destry Rides Again*), and strode downstairs, fingering the pearl-handled Colts. I was shaking. I couldn't believe Ali was so desperate that she would try and smash her way in, but as I reached the hall I was ready for a rock to come splintering through the window.

As I opened the door the knocker came down with another crash – and there was Gran in the porch, clutching her mobile. I'd never seen her so angry.

'*What* are you playing at?' she shouted, striding in, but before I could answer there was an awful wail from the landing, 'Graaan! Granny!' and Rosie came belting down, howling, and threw herself into Gran's arms.

'I thought it was paedophiles!'

You never guess what bogeymen kids dream up for themselves. Even Rosie, when she calmed down, would have to admit that paedophiles generally have more subtle methods than staging an armed attack on a house in broad daylight; but when she was scared out of her wits, and she really had been, that was the worst thing she could think of, getting the paedos mixed up with the vigilantes who go after them. Too much telly.

I took the streaming umbrella and shut the door. Gran had stopped being furious and was sitting on the bottom step, cuddling Rosie.

I said, 'Why were you knocking?'

'I left my key behind,' she said. 'I went out in such a

hurry. When you didn't answer the door I thought something terrible had happened. Then I tried the phone.'

'That was you?'

'And when you didn't answer that either I got really worried. Why didn't you answer the door?'

Over Rosie's head I mouthed, 'I'll tell you later, OK?'

She realized that there had been a good reason so she let it go.

Rosie recovered rapidly once she knew the danger was past. 'Ohmygod! I'm like in the middle of texting Emma. She'll think I'm like dead.'

Normally one of us would have said, 'We should be so lucky,' but we didn't have the heart. Gran stood up and said, 'Clay, a bottle of your father's finest. I'll be down in two minutes.'

She didn't literally mean the finest, which is a case of *Châteauneuf du Pape*, given to Dad by a grateful client, which was lying down in the larder waiting for splendid occasions that hadn't happened yet. But there was some good burgundy in the rack. Dad wouldn't mind us raiding that, it was as much Gran's as his anyway, although he does the choosing. I don't suppose he'd have minded if we'd nicked the *Châteauneuf du Pape*, to be honest.

I took the bottle up to the front room where Gran was ready with two glasses and a corkscrew.

'I suppose I shouldn't encourage you to turn to drink in times of stress,' she said, 'but I'm sure we'll both enjoy it. That cork came out with a healthy plop. Right; cheers! Now, who were you hiding from?'

'I thought it was Ali,' I said.

'Why should Ali come here and try to beat the door down?' Gran said. 'That's my prerogative. Hardly her style.'

'Yes it is,' I said.

'I suppose you were listening in,' Gran said, recalling the conversation with Sandor. 'Well, one glass bowl—'

'It's not one glass bowl,' I said. 'That time at Stitchwort—'

'Penny's place? What happened?'

I hadn't thought, till I overheard the conversation in the front room, that Gran didn't know what had happened at Stitchwort, but evidently Mum hadn't said anything. She'd told me that she didn't think Gran and Dad would want to know. Nobody else had told Gran, why should they? Penny is more Mum's friend than hers, but I'd have to say something now. I did. Gran sat there looking more and more surprised. Then she said, 'But why would Ali come here?'

'Just before you got back John Iverson rang asking for Mum and wanted to know if Penny was here because Ali was looking for her. She'd been round there.'

'At the Iversons'? And you thought that I was Ali trying to batter her way in?'

'She might still come,' I said.

'Are we going to spend the rest of the evening hiding under the bed?'

'Two of us ought to be able to manage,' I said. 'Anyway, why did you go out with Sandor?'

'To keep the silly fool dry,' Gran said.

'Couldn't you just have lent him the umbrella?'

'He was in such a state . . .' Gran muttered. 'I wanted to make sure he got home – well, no, of course he would have got home. But he really must be losing his grip, don't you think, to have come rushing out like that?'

Particularly as his wife was in a car, I thought. 'Had he got his keys?' I said, abandoning all pretence of not having been listening. 'Or had he left the door open?'

'Wide open,' Gran said. 'Fortunately that damn great porch kept the rain out. It's pissing down outside.'

'Don't you think he was . . . overreacting?' I said, cautiously.

'He's under a lot of strain,' Gran said. 'This isn't the first time she's made a dramatic exit. And look what you've just told me about poor Penny. Where's she got this idea about Penny from, anyway?'

'Sandor is rather all over people, isn't he?' I was still being cautious. 'Maybe she gets the wrong impression.' I didn't add that I suspected he wanted her to get the wrong impression. After all, although I suspected it, I couldn't for the life of me think why.

Gran said, 'Does Rosie know who you thought it was?'

'No, I never named names. I wasn't sure . . . I suppose she's up there now, texting her mates about it.'

'If she says anything, let her think it was one of your thwarted boyfriends.'

'She'd never think that. I haven't got any boyfriends.'

'Rosie's fertile imagination will supply one if you drop a hint. For God's sake, who put all that nonsense about paedophiles into her head? *We* haven't encouraged her to think she's at risk every minute of the day, have we? I mean, Anna's brought her up to be sensible, careful; you've all been warned about strange men and cars and chat rooms, but really . . .'

'Yes, but it's not just us, is it? On television, at school – when I was at Grosvenor Road a policewoman used to come and give us chats about road safety. Maybe she does paedophiles now. I suppose we'd better tell Mum and Dad – in case Rosie does say something – no, not Dad.'

'I'll do that,' Gran said. 'Top up? After all, it was me that scared you half to death, wasn't it? And you're right, the less Roger knows about this nonsense, the better.'

'And I scared you. What did you think had happened when I didn't answer the door?'

'I didn't think,' Gran said. 'To start with, I knocked because I assumed you hadn't heard the bell. Then I found the back door was locked as well.'

'That was just chance. We'd been using the French windows all day, remember?'

'And those too; bolted. Jamie being careful for once. And still no one answered. I never got as far as *thinking*, it was gut reaction – something terrible's happened.'

'I didn't think you'd be back so soon.'

'I just wanted to get him out of the house and back

home,' Gran said. 'You're dead right about overreacting. She goes off in a car and he *runs* after her. He didn't even know which way she'd gone.'

'Catching, isn't it?' I said.

'What is?'

'Overreacting. Him, you, me, Rosie—'

'And Ali.'

'We don't know what she overreacted to. Maybe she just reacted.'

'It was some harmless remark about cooking.'

'That's what he says.'

Gran looked at me. 'How do you know – oh, I forget. You heard everything.'

'Not quite everything. I left before the lights went up.'

'Do you think he was lying, then?'

'It's only his version, isn't it? Mum says Ali's got emotional problems. If you ask me, Sandor is Ali's emotional problem.'

'You have to make allowances.' Gran sighed and refilled her glass. She was downing them much faster than me. 'It's his own fault, I suppose; she's much younger than he is, second marriage.'

'Mum's much younger than Dad; second marriage.'

'Very different circumstances. Roger's first wife

died, you know that. And Ali's only half Sandor's age. His first marriage ended in a very bitter divorce, apparently.'

'And whose fault was that?' I growled. I didn't intend to growl, it just came out surly. When had he told her all this? In the front room? Walking up the hill? Or had she found out from Mum?

'Don't be so judgemental. I don't know, but whoever's fault it was, it left scars. He's terrified it will all happen again, that he'll lose Ali because he's handling her all wrong—'

'*Handling* her?'

'Handling the situation. He never knows what kind of a mood she'll be in until he's put his foot in it and then it's too late.'

Like bringing us proteas when he knew she was coming with roses, I thought. 'I wonder how she'd describe it,' I said, but we didn't find out that evening. We stayed up till eleven but no one else came knocking at the door. Jamze got in just before ten and it was about then that Gran rang Sandor to see if Ali had come back, but no one answered so perhaps she had and they were in bed, making up, or she hadn't and he was cantering round the neighbourhood again. No one rang us.

I woke up briefly when Mum and Dad came home, which was unusual. Normally, once I'm asleep nothing wakes me till it's time to get up, unless someone is yelling about the Cona machine right outside the door. I must have been subconsciously on the alert.

I was even more eager than usual to be out of the house early next day. It was not one of those lovely still summer mornings but as chill and blustery as early spring and quite dull because the cloud cover was so low. Postmen had their hoods up against the rain, milkmen scuttled from float to doorstep and back as if they were thieving rather than delivering. It wasn't conducive to a calm contemplative mood and I wasn't in a calm contemplative mood to start with.

Mr Mirza wasn't at the shop. Salman, his eldest son, home from uni, opened the door, looking glum, and told me they'd heard yesterday afternoon that his grandfather had died in Karachi. His parents had managed to get a flight later that day and were frantically getting ready. I said I was sorry.

'It's God's will,' Salman said, with a melancholy shrug.

The Mirzas always say that when something bad happens to them. They have plenty of troubles and they are both so nice and it annoys me that they think it's God's will, when Mr Mirza's unpleasant cousin who runs a letting agency seems to have nothing but good luck which everyone knows he does not deserve; ask his tenants. They don't see it that way, though, and it does seem to help them get through things. Submission: that's what 'Islam' means in Arabic. Perhaps we could do with a bit of submission, I thought, trudging out into the rain again. The Harkers certainly could, instead of taking it out on everyone else.

I looked at their house, looming out of the murk, as I came down Addington Road. Over the low front fence I could see Ali's VW on the gravel in front of the garage at the side. Typical, I thought, his precious Audi has to be tucked up safe. And then I saw that the Audi was parked in the street. I was partly relieved that at least she'd come home last night so we wouldn't have that to worry about, and partly, for a moment, amused because he'd obviously been out when she came home and she'd blocked the access to the garage out of spite: the sort of thing Rosie would do.

As I drew level with the Audi I thought I saw something moving inside it, and veered across the road to have a look, with some vague idea of a cat having got shut in. It wasn't a cat. On the back seat was Sandor, folded up and asleep under a rug. *Then* I knew what had happened: she'd not only blocked the garage entrance, she'd locked him out. If there had been any hammering on doors last night it had been happening here. I couldn't help glancing up at the *Rear Window* window.

There was no one about. I am not proud of what I did next, it was childish, but as everyone else was being childish I thought I might as well join in. It was a trick I picked up from Jake Sorley who once, in a fit of evil, did it down one side of an entire street at two in the morning because all the cars were parked on the pavement (impeding the progress of his bicycle). I brought the flat of my hand down on the bonnet and activated the alarm. It was one of those shrill warbling ones but I didn't wait to see what happened next inside the car. I was high-tailing it for the hills with the whoops of them treacherous redskin critturs ringing in my ears.

They'd never overtake me, though. Once Clay Winchester's got the wind beneath her wings, the Seventh Cavalry couldn't catch up. I could still hear the alarm in the distance from the bottom of the hill.

* * *

I went down to the studio to see if Dad was already up in spite of his late night. As it was the holidays Mum was the only person trying to get out on time; the place was relatively peaceful but I didn't particularly want to talk to her. (I'd cancelled the message from John Iverson because I didn't think he'd like anyone else to hear it, and left Mum a note saying he'd called.) I did not say what he'd called about but I thought she ought to find out what was going on before she heard it in a roundabout way and wondered why I hadn't told her myself. I didn't know if Gran would say anything.

It was all very hole-and-corner. I didn't like that. We never used to keep things from each other – well, of course we did, but not things that involved everybody. And these things shouldn't be involving any of us.

I suppose I ought to have been grateful that Sandor hadn't come back yesterday seeking a bed for the night, but I had a sneaky idea that he rather fancied himself locked out and sleeping in the car; likewise, running coatless through the storm and tempest.

'How was the play?' I said.

'Weird,' Dad said, 'deeply. It was *Titus Andronicus*, which is practically unstagable anyway, given a gangster setting in Old Chicago, which meant that hoods in fedoras were constantly popping up with sub-machine guns remarking, "Aye, marry, 'tis a wonder not to be looked upon." That kind of thing can be very effective but not when it ends with a dinner party where one of the guests is served her own sons in a pie. A horse's head in the bed is one thing – speaking of which, what was going on here last night?'

As this had nothing to do with horses in the bed I didn't see it coming.

'Nothing – much,' I said.

'Don't get shifty,' Dad said, and he was looking irritable. Dad, irritable with me? Me, being shifty with Dad? 'Something upset Rosie,' he said. 'I mean *really* upset.'

'Don't tell me she's awake already? In the holidays?'

'She was up last night. When we got back, quarter to one, she came creeping down the stairs in a panic because she thought someone was breaking in. She was half asleep, couldn't get much sense out of her, but she was going on about Marina getting locked out and banging on the door because you wouldn't let her in. Doesn't sound like you, Clay.'

I gave one second's consideration to the thwarted boyfriend scenario that Gran had pitched, and rejected it instantly. Dad knew me better than that.

'I thought it was Ali Harker,' I said.

'You were hiding from Ali Harker – the pocket wife? Does she think you have designs on the god-like Sandor?'

'Dad, it's not funny.' I was just about the only person she didn't suspect of having designs upon Sandor, but once I'd said that I had to explain to him why it wasn't funny and out it all came: Sandor's visit last night, Ali's outburst in the shop, John Iverson's phone call. It got less funny the more I let out. Dad began to look confused and I began to think that he hadn't known about any of it. I tried to lighten the mood towards the end.

'Anyway, Ali did come home – her home – last night while Sandor was looking for her, I suppose. She's locked him out and he's sleeping in the Audi, in the street. Well, I should think he's got up by now.' I omitted my part in Sandor's getting up.

Dad sat at his desk, head propped on hand, staring out of the window at the back of the house. After a while he said, 'I know I must seem a bit out of the way, stuck down here, but do you mean all this has been going on without my knowing anything about it?'

'I don't think anyone knows everything,' I said carefully. 'I think we're all sort of trying not to betray each other's confidences.'

'Confidences?' he shouted. 'As in *confidential* – private, secret? Why don't they book a hall, sell tickets. I never have enjoyed audience participation. If those two idiots want to break up in public, fine. I'm happy to watch from the back row of the one and nines. But I don't see why the rest of us should have to join in.'

'You haven't had to join in,' I muttered.

He looked thoughtful. 'No, I've been kept right out of it, haven't I?'

'Perhaps it's more a woman thing?'

'Sandor H is certainly a woman thing.'

'Don't tell Mum I told you,' I said.

'Do you mean to say, I'm supposed to pretend I don't know?'

'Does it make any difference that you do know?'

He said, 'Look, Clay, there's no reason at all, *as far as I can see*, why I shouldn't know.'

'I don't want Mum to think I've been blabbing.'

'As far as I can see,' he had said. What I hadn't mentioned was Mum and Rosie meeting Sandor in Pizzacato and possibly at other times. 'He's always here,' Rosie had said, but knowing Rosie that could have meant twice, or even just the once.

'She won't think you've been blabbing,' Dad said. 'I'll just make casual enquiries from Rosie or Marina about last night's shenanigans. That would be reasonable, wouldn't it?'

Yes, of course it would be reasonable. Gran might even raise the subject herself.

'Watch out for the Canadians,' he called out as I went back up the garden.

What were we all *doing*? I wondered. Why don't we all know what we are all doing? When I went in Mum, who ought to have been leaving for work, was on the phone – to John Iverson I gathered, after a couple of sentences. She must have come down and seen my note, or seen it when she got in last night. It had been too late to do anything about it then.

She was saying, 'Ali seems to have got entirely the wrong end of the stick – well, just about every stick, by the sound of it . . . No, I haven't spoken to anyone yet, we didn't get in till almost one . . . If Clay says he was with Marina then he must have been . . . You surely don't think—'

I closed the kitchen door so as not to hear any more. What was it that John Iverson surely didn't think? That I'd been lying last night when I rang him, giving Sandor a false alibi? How could John think that? I'd known him – he'd known me – since I was a baby. And he hardly knew Sandor at all, but he was ready to believe I was lying. I wanted to storm out into the hall, like Rosie but full of righteous wrath instead of some imagined grievance, grab the handset and give him a good bollocking down the line.

But I didn't. I just sat in the kitchen feeling miserable. Whatever was going on was getting to all of us, even Rosie. But not, so far as I knew, to Jamze. What would it take for Jamze to notice what was going on, much less be affected by it? As far as Jamze was concerned, Sandor was still that geezer on the doorstep and I was sure he'd never met Ali at all.

I could hear Mum still talking out in the hall although I couldn't make out the words, and this time I wasn't trying to, but from the way her voice was coming and going I could tell that she was pacing up and down. This was something we try not to do with that particular phone because it picks up interference and to the person at the other end it sounds as though you are being buzzed by light aircraft or industrial-strength mosquitoes. I wondered if John's phone was also cordless. If he was walking about too it would sound like an aerial dogfight.

I was glad I could still think of something silly.

Then Mum was suddenly back in the kitchen. She

saw me sitting there looking fed up and said, 'What's the matter? Has something happened?'

Has something happened?

I said, 'Mr Mirza's father died. He's got to fly to Karachi.'

She said, 'Oh, that's sad,' vaguely. She didn't know the Mirzas because our own paper shop is the one at the end of the street. She took a deep breath and said, 'I gather there was a bit of a mix-up last night.'

'Those old crossed wires again?' I said nastily.

She looked taken aback. 'There seems to have been a misunderstanding . . .'

'Oh, *yes*. We only had Sandor here looking for Ali, and John Iverson ringing up looking for Sandor.'

'Darling, he was looking for Penny.'

'Same thing, isn't it?' I snapped. 'And I heard you on the phone just now. Does he think I was lying? What does Penny say? Does he think she's been lying too?'

'Of course he doesn't think you've been lying, but when he tried ringing the Harkers last night, no one answered.'

'Have you spoken to Gran?' I said, needing to know more before I said anything else.

'She's not up yet.'

'Ask her what happened. Maybe she'll lie too.'

169

'Clay!'

'Well, no one's above suspicion at the moment, are they? Sandor came here looking for Ali, *so he said*. Gran went back with him and then came straight home again. She rang later too and there wasn't any answer. Check with her. Sandor must have gone out again.'

'But where's Ali gone?'

'She hasn't gone anywhere. She's back home. I saw her car as I went past just now. And the Audi's there too.' I didn't let on that Sandor had been kipping in it.

'But why wouldn't you let Mum in last night? Rosie was having nightmares . . .'

'I didn't know it was Gran, I thought it was Ali. And after what she did in the shop I didn't want her in here.'

'Why should Ali come here?' Mum was beginning to look bewildered. Just catching up with the rest of us.

'I don't know, why should Sandor come here? Next time, I shan't let him in, either.'

'Clay, what's got into you?'

'What's got into *me*? Nothing. This is nothing to do with me. It's nothing to do with any of us, is it? Don't you see enough of him at work?'

'See *enough* of him? I hardly ever see him, he's not

in my department. He's not even in the same building. It was sheer chance that we got introduced that first time.'

'*What* first time?'

'Don't pounce like that. One of our senior managers brought him in at lunch, showing him round; he'd just joined the firm, remember? He mentioned that they were new to the area and didn't know anybody locally, and I said they must come round for a meal. If he'd sat at another table for lunch we wouldn't even have got that far.'

Small beginnings.

'Then why have they latched on to us like this?'

'They haven't latched on.'

'He has. And what about the Iversons?'

'I don't know. I don't know what's going on there,' Mum said, miserably.

'You think something is going on?'

'Perhaps they think something's going on here.'

'Perhaps there is.'

Oh, God, I shouldn't have said that. Mum looked as if I'd hit her but having said it there was no point in letting it go to waste. 'Rosie said he's always round here.'

'Clay, he's not.'

'What about at Pizzacato, Rosie's birthday?'

'What about it?'

'You met him there.'

'Met him? He came in while I was paying the bill. He joined us for coffee. You don't think I'd arranged it, do you?'

'I don't know. *Does* he come round here?'

'Once or twice, you know that. Rosie may have seen him then.'

As I'd suspected, 'always' meant 'more than never'.

'Why does he come here?' And does Dad know? I wanted to ask, but didn't.

'To talk,' Mum said. 'You can't imagine how unhappy all this is making him.'

'All what?'

'With Ali.'

'Isn't it making her unhappy? Does she know he comes here?'

Mum said, 'Clay, he hasn't come here often enough to make her unhappy.'

'Just once would do it.' I was growling again.

'She's so suspicious, jealous, and there's nothing to be jealous or suspicious of.'

'Isn't there?'

'He adores her.'

'Does he?' I said. 'I wouldn't want to be adored like that.'

It was after this that I began to ask myself if perhaps Mum knew even less than the rest of us.

Six

Before Gran came to live with us we all used to go on holiday together. The fact that we didn't any more wasn't because of Gran, it was mainly on account of Jamze being BORED and EMBARRASSED by our company, sending out great tentacles of boredom and embarrassment like a big sulky octopus. When Rosie started to get in on the act Mum and Dad gave up the idea of family holidays, and with Gran taking turns at going away, there was always someone at home to keep an eye on the house and anyone (Jamze) who didn't want to go anywhere with anybody.

This year Rosie was taken to France with her friend Emma. She and Emma probably spent the whole three weeks sitting on a bed squeezing each other's zits. After she got back I asked her where they'd been. Rosie boiled over. 'God, that's all I get all the time, where did you go, what did you do, who were you with? Just get off my case. Right?'

'I wondered if you'd had a nice time,' I said.

'No you didn't, you hope I had a horrible time. You're only happy when I'm miserable.'

'That's right, work it out. I'm delirious twenty-four/seven.'

I went to Devon with Mum and Dad and we saw a lot of sheep and buzzards and no one mentioned the Harkers once. If they were still speaking to each other, I thought they'd go somewhere like Tuscany – well, I couldn't quite see Sandor clubbing in Ayia Napa. When we came home it was Gran's turn. She was off to see a friend in Oregon. I've always loved the sound of Oregon, not just because of the Oregon Trail, the two thousand miles from Missouri that the pioneers travelled. She'd been there before and brought back photographs of a beautiful coastline and of her friend Beatrice who is the same age and wears her hair in two long grey plaits down past her waist so that she looks like a Native American. They camp out and have fires on the beach and I dream that one day Gran will ask me to go with her. I never mention it though because this is the only time she gets to see Beatrice. I don't think I'd spoil it for them but I wouldn't want to chance it.

Gran left two days after we got back from Devon.

Dad drove her to Heathrow. Mum did a huge wash and iron of all the stuff we'd brought home and I spent an afternoon making lovely salads for supper.

I hadn't given the Harkers a thought while I was in Devon. The last morning I did the paper round before we went away I'd noticed, for the sixth day running, that there were no bottles in the porch of 107 Addington Road, and the front downstairs curtains were drawn. There might be three explanations: a) they were on holiday together or apart, b) they had left each other simultaneously like Daisy and her bloke or c) they were dead and peacefully bloating in the summer heat. I ruled out c) on the grounds that the bottles weren't piling up, although I was sorry to see how wilted the flowers were in the balcony tubs. After that they went out of my mind; it was only passing the house every morning that made me think of them, anyway.

We laid the table on the paving outside the French windows – it was too hot to eat indoors, even in the evenings. Mum had wine cooling in the fridge and made spritzers. Dad collared Jamze on his way down from the bathroom and I brought out the food.

Jamze looked at the table and was visibly moved. 'Cool,' he said and fell into a chair. This was high praise from Jamze but the table did look nice, the garden was green and bright and you couldn't hear anyone's stereo, not even the tinny percussion from Jamze's Walkman. Dad had politely asked him to remove it from his ears while we ate.

We passed round the salad bowls and I was just thinking, How civilized this is, and trying *not* to think, Especially without Rosie, who wouldn't be back for another week, when the phone rang.

Mum: Bugger.

Dad: Who the hell's that?

Jamze: (Fondling his mobile which lies close by on the table) It won't be for me.

Clay: I'll get it.

Dad: Let it ring. They can leave a message.

We all spoke more or less at the same moment so it was only on its fourth ring when Mum, who was nearest the windows, stood up and said, 'I'd better get it.'

That was fine by Jamze who, having touched his mobile, had gone into automatic texting mode. Dad and I went on serving. We were all so relaxed I don't think it occurred to anyone who it *might* be.

Mum didn't come back.

'Bet it's Marina,' Dad said. 'Flight's delayed – been cancelled. Wings fell off. Maybe she'll get the bus back. Oh well, might as well start. At least it can't get cold.'

I couldn't hear Mum's voice. Whoever was on the other end was doing most of the talking.

After about ten minutes Dad said, 'It can't be Marina, unless she's bobbing about on a life raft in the mid-Atlantic.'

'You can phone from planes, these days,' I said. 'Why doesn't Mum say she's in the middle of supper.'

'Oh, you know Anna,' Dad said. 'Some friend telling her every thrilling detail of their cruise around the Humber estuary and she'll just stand there saying, "Yes . . . yes . . . ye-e-e-es," sounding utterly fascinated instead of yawning audibly until they take the hint and hang up.'

At last she came back just as James was getting up to go and Dad was letting him because socially it made no difference whether Jamze was there or not. She came through the French windows passing Jamze on the way, and sat down looking rather bewildered.

'That was Sandor,' she said, and took a swig at her spritzer which was going a bit flat. 'She's left him.'

There was a short pause and then Dad said, 'Why do we have to know that?'

Another pause.

'I suppose he felt he had to tell somebody,' Mum said, and started to eat. All that listening had given her an appetite.

'It took you about five seconds to tell us,' Dad said. 'What took him twenty minutes?'

'He was, well, pouring it all out,' Mum said. 'Apparently they had a terrible time on holiday.'

'Tuscany?' Dad said, and I thought, Snap!

'Yes, near Siena. He hoped it would be a chance to get away and sort things out but it seems—'

'Why should it make any difference where they went?' Dad said. 'If they can't stand the sight of each other in England, being stuck in a barn with no running water half-way up an Appennine won't make things any easier.'

'They went there on their honeymoon,' Mum said.

Dad said, 'Some people never learn.'

Mum said, 'He's coming round here.'

'What, *now*?'

'In about half an hour.'

'Did we come back from Devon for this?' Dad said. 'Half an hour? Didn't you tell him we were eating?'

'That would have sounded unsympathetic. It won't take half an hour. You're all finished.'

'I rather fancied staying out here, lingering over the wine and olives, watching the sun go down,' Dad said. 'As one does in Tuscany.'

'Well, we can,' Mum said. 'Sandor can join us. I'll get more wine.'

'Think he'll need lubricating?' Dad said. 'Forget it. The man can run on empty. He's a *raconteur*. He'll have plenty to *raconte* – if he hasn't said it all already. Not that that will stop him saying it all again.'

Dad evidently hadn't forgotten that first time the Harkers had come to dinner and Sandor had sat at the end of the table where *he* ought to have been, holding forth. I hadn't known he'd minded so much. I thought it was only me.

'I'll take him into the front room, then,' Mum said, still looking bewildered and now hurt as well.

'No need,' Dad said, getting up. He'd cleaned his plate but his glass was still half full. He didn't take it with him. 'I've got things to do.'

He went down the garden to the studio. Mum went on eating and didn't say anything. I took some more salad to keep her company.

'Do you want another spritzer?' I said.

'I'll wait till Sandor gets here.'

'What does he want to tell you,' I asked, 'that he didn't say on the phone?'

'Oh, don't *you* start,' Mum snapped, and I remembered that this was more or less what Dad had said. 'He just wants someone to talk to.'

'Shall I stay?' I thought it might be easier for her. I know what it's like when people start pouring out their sorrows – in kitchens, at parties.

'No thanks, there's no need for that . . . thanks, anyway.'

Which was fine by me. I didn't particularly want to stay. The evening wasn't going to turn out as we'd planned – not that we had planned anything, we hardly ever do. It had just seemed so promising . . . I cleared the table, washed up, put another bottle in the fridge and went upstairs.

From my window I could see right down the garden into the studio. Dad wasn't at his desk but the interior of the shed was flickering. He was watching a tape, black and white; I guessed one of our Westerns. It can get stuffy in the shed and my room was airy, but I almost decided to go down and join him.

Then I thought, Maybe he won't want me to. He

wouldn't say that, of course, but if he wasn't in the mood for company I'd know.

How would I know? I wasn't company, I was Clay. Never had I known Dad not want me around. Or Mum, come to that. I'd always known that there were times when it was better not to be around for their sake – or mine; first thing in the morning, for instance. I hated this sense of not being sure, being afraid of finding out how it might feel to be not wanted.

Coffee! The cure all. I'd make coffee and take some to Dad.

But suppose he said, 'I can make my own coffee if I want it, thank you very much.'

He'd never ever said anything like that to me, but then I'd never heard him talk to Mum the way he had this evening. They'd always had their separate friends and were often mildly rude about them to each other, but Dad had sounded really hostile. I wished Gran was there to take the heat off. She must still be airborne. I couldn't remember where she would have to change planes – Boston or Washington or LA.

The flickering in the shed grew quite agitated, most likely an Indian attack or a cavalry charge, or both if it was *They Died With Their Boots On* which is about Custer's Last Stand. It was made in 1945 before people began to admit that General George Armstrong Custer had been asking for everything he'd got. It was so simple once; black hats for the bad guys, white hats for the goodies; black and white hats for black and white movies. You didn't have to worry about motivation or what made people tick, you knew who was good and bad, you didn't have to wonder why. You could even tell by the actors. The biggest surprise in *Once Upon a Time in the West* is seeing all-time good guy Henry Fonda on screen and realizing that he is one of the heavies, one of the bad bastards, as Dad calls them, when he means seriously vile.

Colour did that; made you wonder. Gran says something similar about horror films – for the opposite reason; colour took all the subtlety out of them and paved the way for slasher movies. If you can show red blood you might as well have lots of it, full colour evisceration – and there's nothing so red as Technicolor.

Personally I think that only someone like Gran could find *Night of the Living Dead* subtle, but I know what she means. Colour leaves so little to the imagination.

We needn't have broken up our supper in such a hurry; it was at least another hour before the doorbell rang.

Mum didn't take Sandor into the front room. As

we'd all abandoned the table by the French windows they sat out there. My window is immediately above it, and it was open. I didn't close it.

It was much too hot to sit indoors with a closed window.

Mum was saying, 'When did you find out?'

Sandor: When we got home.

Mum: Home from where?

Sandor: From Italy.

Mum: Didn't you come back together?

Sandor: (Muffled – with anguish?) Gatwick – at the baggage claim. We were together at the carousel, her bag came round and I put it on the trolley, then when I stepped forward to get the other – they'd got separated – she went. I looked round, she'd taken the trolley and gone. (I can just picture that, Ali fleeing like Cinderella at midnight through the green channel, scattering customs officials)

Mum: Did you have a quarrel on the plane?

Sandor: That was the final one. It never stopped after we got to the villa.

Clay: (Aside) Oh, a *villah*, of course. Not a barn with no running water.

Mum: (Gently) What made you go away when things were so – so—

Sandor: I thought, if we could be alone, just as we were at the beginning, we could work things out. I'd even tried to rent the same villa.

Mum: The same as the honeymoon one? Was that a good idea?

Sandor: Probably not – but I couldn't get it anyway – such short notice. Ali wanted to go to Greece.

Clay: So you took her to Italy. Smart move, wise-guy.

Sandor: I thought . . . I thought . . . we could somehow recapture . . . I'm a hopeless romantic, I know . . . I kept hoping . . .

I looked out of the window. They were sitting at the table, heads close together.

I wondered how they looked from the studio and if Dad could see.

Although I had nothing in particular to do, I got itchy with resentment at all the things I couldn't do: couldn't go and watch telly – not with Sandor emoting a few metres away; couldn't sit in the garden for the same reason; couldn't go down to the studio. That is, I *could* do any of those things but I knew it would be better if I didn't. Daisy was on holiday in Greece with her mum and her mum's newest new bloke. I was just thinking of going for a late bike ride – it was the time of year for long mellow twilights – when the phone rang.

My first reaction was, Oh, please, not Ali, but I thought I'd better get it in case Sandor was in the middle of saying something heart-rending. I zipped along to Mum's room.

It was Gran calling from Chicago where her connecting flight had been delayed. She didn't seem to mind, it was only three thirty in the afternoon there. Once, when she used to ring us transatlantic, we got strange hiccoughs and echoes on the line and two people speaking at once. Now she sounded as if she was making a local call.

'Having a lovely evening?' she said. 'Roger was making plans for a midnight feast on the lawn by the sound of it. I asked if he'd just been waiting for me to go before letting rip.'

'Don't be daft,' I said. 'We could have let rip in Devon.'

'Well, *are* you having a lovely evening?'

'We were,' I said, 'but Sandor Harker came round.'

'Not chasing Ali, again?' Gran said.

'No, she's left him.'

'When?'

'I dunno. Gatwick. He's telling Mum all about it downstairs. D'you want to speak to her?'

'I'd hate to break up the party,' Gran said. 'What's Roger doing, taking notes?'

'In the studio.'

'Safest place – oh, my flight's just come up. I'll ring you tomorrow. Enjoy what's left of the evening – watch *Dracula*. There's a fellow in that called Harker.'

'He's the hero, not the vampire,' I said, but she'd gone. Off to Oregon.

I thought of Dad in the studio. It hadn't crossed my mind that he'd been looking forward to his evening all day, and now it was spoiled.

There were bottles again in the porch at 107, but only one of each, milk and juice. Sometimes the curtains were drawn, sometimes open, and someone was keeping the hedge trimmed but I didn't imagine it was Sandor. He'd get a man in. The plants on the balcony had died in the heat.

I could see this much as I came down the hill each morning, from 66 (*Telegraph* and *Mail*), 72 (*Financial Times* and *Guardian*) and 84 (*Independent*). As I went by though, I never looked up or across the road to where the Audi now stood alone on the gravel outside the garage.

Rosie was due back at the end of the week. No one said, 'Let's have one last meal in peace without being accused of trying to poison anybody or make them obese or ruin their entire lives by giving them a funny look at the wrong moment,' but when Dad announced, 'The spinach is getting out of hand and I'd hate to see it going to waste. Slugs have died for that spinach,' Mum said, 'Let's have a soufflé.'

Soufflé aux épinards leaves Rosie cold ('It's got *bits* in it') but I like making it. Hardly anyone has soufflés these days, Gran says, on account of microwaves. I don't know if you can nuke a soufflé but I wouldn't like to try and anyway, the fun is knowing that it's in the oven and you've just got to trust it because you dare not open the door to see how it is coming along in case it collapses. But if you know what you are doing, and I do, you don't keep opening the oven door to look and it comes out beautifully fluffy and golden and everyone is impressed.

The other hazard is the people who are going to eat it. Ideally everyone has to be at the table before it goes into the oven because, according to Gran again, domestic incidents used to flare up over soufflés spoiled because guests were late; cooks gave notice; marriages foundered. Perhaps it's just as well they have gone out of fashion, although in fact they are very easy to make. It's the timing.

So I waited until Mum was home from work before I even started it, because once you've started you can't stop. I heard her come in and have some sort of one-sided exchange with Jamze in the hall, so I got going. Then she came through the kitchen on her way down to see Dad in the studio which made me think, in passing, that once, not so long ago, Dad was almost always in the house when Mum came home.

I pointed meaningly at the soufflé dish and said, 'Seven thirty sharp; OK, lady?'

'You're the cook,' she said and I got on with it.

I didn't notice how long she was in the studio but my precious creation was in the oven when she came through again.

'Fifteen minutes,' I said.

'I'll be straight down.' She was going for the stairs but she paused at the foot and said, 'Any messages?'

'I haven't checked. No one's rung since I got in.'

'I'll just see,' she said, running up.

I went after her.

'*Mum*. The soufflé. Can't it wait till after?'

'Oh, I won't make any calls,' she said.

'If you do I'll come and *drag* you down. You know I can.'

I looked in the back room to make sure that Jamze was where he ought to be. I'd already laid the table and he was in his place, communicating on autopilot. I went to the French windows and semaphored to Dad who had come out of the studio and was round at the side of it, inspecting the vegetable strip where he'd picked the spinach for me. Even though it takes a lot for four there was plenty left. Rosie might yet be forced to ingest some.

'Ten minutes! Go and get washed!'

He saluted, US Cavalry fashion, and came towards the house. Wow! Did I have everyone under control? Actually I had been lying, there was still a quarter of an hour to go but I wasn't taking any chances.

At twenty-five past I called up to Mum and she didn't answer. I could see the bathroom door from the foot of the stairs and it was open, so she wasn't showering – the usual excuse if anyone is pretending not to hear. 'I was in the shower,' they tell you, wide-eyed and bone dry.

'*Mum!*'

'Just a minute.' She sounded muffled so her door, which I couldn't see, must be shut.

'*The soufflé.*'

This time she didn't answer and I couldn't hear footsteps. But I could smell a soufflé with only moments to go.

A base suspicion came over me. The hall phone was barely a metre away. I could see Dad in the kitchen washing his hands at the sink. I went up three stairs, sat down, and put my arm through the banisters. The telephone table is exactly level with the fourth step and very carefully I lifted the handset, mindful of the low-flying-aircraft effect. When I put it to my ear I heard exactly what I expected to hear: Sandor's voice saying, 'It's as if I can't bear to let anyone know I'm there. I draw the curtains and sit in the dark—'

I wanted to slam the phone down or, to be accurate, to hurl it down the hall Ali-fashion so that it hit the front door. But I didn't. I was feeling bad enough about what I was doing without letting on that I was doing it. I put the handset down gently and withdrew my hand just as Dad came up the steps from the kitchen calling, 'Clay! You haven't *forgotten* it, have you?'

'Just coming.'

I went into the kitchen just as he went into the back

room and raised some kind of a response from Jamze ('Put that bloody thing down for five minutes.' 'Hanh?').

Half past; the soufflé was done, I knew it was; I'd timed it, I could smell it. I heard it calling from the oven: 'Get me out of here.'

The plates were hot, the side salad and rolls were ready on the table and so were we ready; Dad and Jamze in the back room, me in the oven gloves, poised.

I let a minute go by, then another, then I turned off the gas and opened the oven door. The soufflé was perfect, one more minute though and it would have started to scorch. I yelled, 'Coming through!' and bore it into the back room and put it on the serving mat. Jamze whipped his mobile out of the way just in time. It did look good; we sat and gazed at it, me, Dad and Jamze; and gazed. It seemed to me that it was beginning to go down very slightly.

Dad said, 'Where's Anna?'

I said, 'She swore she'd be down on time – she'll be here in a moment,' but it was already past time. It was silly, I was so hurt, not because Mum was late but because of why she was late. She knew how important the timing was and she'd been home, in the house, she'd said she wouldn't call anyone but she had to make an exception for this – this *nuisance* who was more important than her own daughter.

Oh, that was ridiculous, I know, but I didn't know it then, that she'd been so disturbed by the impassioned message he'd left that she had called to say she would ring him later and then couldn't shut him up. I just sat staring at my collapsing soufflé and wanted to cry, like Calamity Jane going all girlie.

'Don't let's sit here and watch it deflate,' Dad said. 'Will you cut it, Clay, or shall I?'

'You do it,' I said, and Dad made a sort of respectful ritual gesture with the serving spoon as if propitiating it (Oh, soufflé, for what I am about to do to you, forgive me) and plunged in. Steam gushed from its hot, rich heart like a volcano about to blow and Dad served us a quarter each, leaving one reproachful peak in the dish for Mum, but already it was ceasing to be a peak.

We helped ourselves to salad.

And then Mum came down, I heard her hurrying on the stairs, along the hall, but I didn't turn when she came in at the door with a wail of sorrow.

'Oh, Clay, the soufflé. I'm sorry.'

'No point in waiting,' Dad said. 'What kept you?'

I felt my fists clenching and an argument broke out

in my head. *'Don't* tell him. Let's just eat.' 'Don't lie to him.'

I said, 'Were you on the phone? I thought you said—'

'Oh, Sandor left a message – I had to get back to him. I only meant to take a minute.'

I didn't say anything.

Dad said, 'Why?'

Mum still wasn't getting it. 'Oh, you know what a mess he's in. Apparently Ali sent a solicitor's letter full of accusations and demands and he's – I don't know – gathering support. He's getting a bit intense. "Those who are not for me are against me," he said.'

'Who does he think he is?' Dad asked. 'George W. Bush? Was all this in the message?'

'No – he just sounded so desolate I had to ring back and once he'd started talking—'

'You could have hung up,' I said. 'You could have told him about the soufflé.'

'I am so sorry about the soufflé, Clay. It's wonderful. But you didn't hear him.'

I couldn't tell her that I had.

'Do you know what he told me? He got a bottle of Ali's scent that she'd left behind and poured it into the washing machine on a rinse cycle and then washed all the sheets.'

'What, so that he could be permanently enfolded in essence of Ali?' Dad said. 'Night and morn, a lungful of the departed.'

'Roger!'

'Isn't that rather an intimate kind of thing to be broadcasting?'

'Smell is the most nostalgic sense.'

'True, but that's his problem, not ours.'

Jamze growled, 'Wanker.'

We all stopped eating and stared at him, not just in amazement that he'd said anything but in amazement that he'd even been listening. I suspected that at least two of us agreed with him, but Mum looked really shocked.

'Jamie! You don't know anything about him.'

Jamze did not look up. He bent low over his plate and shovelled food into his mouth as if he was stoking his fire, but he didn't stop talking. I was quite glad that he hadn't looked up.

'Yeah, dead right I don't know anything about him, I'm just sick of *hearing* about him, stupid poncy name, what is he, a power tool, why's he always ringing up and coming round and spoiling things, never even met him—'

'Yes you have,' I said, wanting to slow him down

even if I couldn't stop him. 'You let him in, twice. Or rather, you left him on the doorstep twice.'

'*That* dickhead? What's he coming here for, then? Having it off with Mum?'

Mum and I howled '*No!*' Dad said nothing.

'What's he after, then? I don't want to know about his fucking bedsheets.' By this time Jamze had his face down almost in his plate. I couldn't see his expression but his ears and the back of his neck were glowing.

'Jamie, give it a rest,' Dad said.

'Give it a rest? That's good coming from you. What do *you* want him here for? I mean, what's going on? What's going *on*?'

'Just leave it, will you?' Dad said.

Mum should have taken that advice. She said, 'Jamie, nothing's going on. You're imagining it.'

Bad move. Jamze erupted.

'What's it all about then? Why's everyone in such a foul mood all the time? You think I'm stupid or something, you think I can't tell? All this – this – this *stuff*—'

Then he did what Rosie does, leaped up, slammed down his fork and scrambled out of the room.

Mum started to go after him. 'Jamie, wait. Where are you going?'

He yelled back, 'Who cares where I'm going? I don't!'

The front door slammed. Mum was already in the hall; she didn't come back.

Dad and I sat at the table with the remains of the soufflé that Mum hadn't eaten, the wreck of the salad and Jamze's mobile, lying by his plate vibrating mournfully.

'Well,' Dad said, 'he won't go far without that.'

I'd been thinking the same thing; the mobe was Jamze's life support system. As soon as he realized he'd left it behind his thoughts would turn homeward even if he didn't. I doubted if he'd get even as far as the main road.

Dad reached across and put his hand on my arm – not something he often does, none of us does. We aren't all that touchy-feely; it never seems necessary.

'That was a rotten return for all your hard work,' he said. 'I'm sorry.'

'Not your fault,' I said. We both knew that.

He poked at Mum's bit of soufflé. 'No point in keeping it warm, I suppose.'

'Not really. It's past saving.'

'I'd better go and see ... I was going to do the washing up but ...'

'No, don't worry. I'll do it.'

'Leave it till—'

'No, it's cool. I'll do it. You know how anything with cheese in it sticks.'

From force of habit he turned left at the door to go down to the studio by way of the kitchen, then remembered where he was supposed to be going and turned right along the hall towards the stairs. I cleared the plates, threw the remains of the rolls out for the birds, sluiced the soufflé down the sink and took the remains of the salad out to the compost heap because it had been already dressed and was starting to turn to bitter mush.

The compost heap is behind the studio, past the spinach, Dad's end of the garden, Dad's bolthole. Perhaps he was feeling that he had been bolting too often. I didn't mean to criticize but he did tend to slide away from things.

And what was Jamze feeling? I'd been right when I thought that he'd notice if the safety net was taken away. There he'd been, peacefully swinging from branch to branch through the leaf canopy of his private jungle and then something had made him look down and he'd seen how far away the ground was and that there was nothing between him and it.

And what had made him look down? Sandor Harker.

One of Gran's metaphor theories is that vampire stories stem from a fear of venereal infection which was just about incurable in the nineteenth century. Wasn't Sandor infecting everything he touched, like a vampire? But why did he have to infect us? Dad had said that he was quite happy to watch from the back row of the one and nines; one shilling and ninepence in the currency they used when he was young, the most expensive seats in the cinema stalls. They didn't show films much on telly then and videos hadn't been invented, much less DVDs. If we don't like what we are watching on the box we switch over or switch off. Why couldn't we switch Sandor off when we'd had enough? We'd all had enough, even Mum. Dad had had enough on the very first night we met him.

What had happened this evening wouldn't have happened if Gran had been there. I wished she'd ring but I knew she wouldn't. The last time she'd called she said that she and Beatrice were going to the beach for a few days. I pictured them sitting by their fire on the sand, next to the Pacific Ocean, under a sky full of stars, drinking wine, happily smoking whatever they were smoking. I wanted to be there, not with Gran, to be Gran, to have jumped half a century, not looking forward to all the things I would be able to do but looking back on all the things I had done, without having to have done them.

That would be cheating. Gran said she'd earned the right to do what she liked without caring what anyone else thought. And she *had* earned it. The joke about running off to a tepee in Wales, even if it was a caravan in Shropshire, wasn't really a joke. When she was at university she found she was pregnant, and her parents were very sympathetic until they found out that she and her boyfriend didn't intend to marry or even stay together. They thought she would have the baby adopted and when she refused they told her not to come home until she changed her mind, and she never did. Never changed her mind and never went home again. Mum didn't know her grandparents and the man we'd always called Grandad wasn't, in fact, our grandfather. Mum was three when Gran married him. By then she managed to get a teaching qualification and was working and everything was fine.

But the joke about the bridge players wasn't all that funny either. Mum said he'd been a wonderful father to her but she often wondered if the reason he'd been happy to take her on was because he couldn't have any children of his own. He'd had mumps when he was thirteen and it had left him sterile. There was no IVF treatment or sperm donation then. As well as being an accountant he was an amateur athlete and full of energy, and they'd travelled all over the place on holidays while Mum was growing up – and then he started playing bridge. Mum said it transformed him, it was almost as if he were addicted – well, I suppose he was. Gran stayed with him, bored out of her skull, for five years, until he died – of monomania, Gran said, but it was a heart attack. I can remember him up to the time I was about eight, being all the things Mum said he was, a wonderful grandfather the way he'd been a wonderful father, and then they went to the Isle of Wight and after that I can't remember him at all. He switched himself off.

After he died Gran discovered that it hadn't just been bridge. One thing had led to another, poker, casinos, he'd been gambling heavily, that was the monomania, the addiction. He'd run up hideous debts and remortgaged the house without telling her. She was left with nothing. We didn't talk about these things, we just knew them, they were Gran's back story, and Mum's; the things that had made them what they were. It was no good wishing that I could skip all that, I'd never be anything, never become anything. I'd have to live my own back story.

But Sandor didn't seem to have one at all, it was as if he had to keep reminding people that he was there, reminding them that he was real. I wasn't at all sure he was real. Next time I saw him, I told myself, lingering beside the compost heap, I must look in the mirror to see if he had a reflection.

Which was the sort of thing that normally I'd have said to Dad and we'd have had a laugh about it.

The worst thing was, I hadn't made the soufflé just to use up the spinach. It was meant to be a celebration. I'd picked up my GCSE results that morning, two Bs and nine As, and I was going to announce them after supper: Look what Clever Clay's done, ta-rah! Later I left them on the hall table for people to find and they did, next morning, and everyone felt terrible, especially Mum. No more terrible than I did, though.

Rosie came back, Gran came back, Dad went away for a few days.

I was in the front room when I saw Rosie climb out of Emma's mother's car. She was brown and smiling and she and Emma were shrieking at each other while

Emma's mum got the luggage out of the boot and our mum went out to thank her and ask her in for coffee. I could see by the way the conversation was going that Emma's mum didn't have time because they'd dropped Rosie off on the way back from Dover without going home first. I also saw Rosie's expression change as she came up the steps. She stopped bouncing and started to slouch; the corners of her mouth turned down.

I don't know, perhaps I had some idea of trying to hint that it would be a sensible move to keep up the happy-child act for a bit longer in the present climate; instead of following Mum out to pick up the bags I stopped in the hall and beckoned to Rosie.

'Whaaaat?'

'Did you have a nice time?'

'What's that smell?'

'I don't know – Toilet Duck, I expect. I've been cleaning the bathroom.'

'That is *so* disgusting.'

'You prefer it septic? *Did* you have a nice time?' But she was already on her way upstairs. I could tell by her elbows that she was texting.

Mum dumped the bags in the hall and closed the front door. She'd heard.

'Yes, she had a lovely time; Helen says they never stopped eating and never stopped screaming. I don't know how lovely that was for her. Rosie!'

'Whaaaat?'

'Could you come back down for a moment?'

'Whyyyy?'

'Never mind the whys. Come down.'

We could hear the exasperated sigh all the way from the attic.

After a while Rosie reappeared on the landing. '*Now* what?'

'You might say hullo.'

'I *did* say hullo, I said it when you came out, if you hadn't been talking to *her* you'd of heard me, I can't do anything right, I've only just got back and you're like on at me already.'

'I'm not on at you. I asked you to come downstairs, that's all.'

'After I'd got *all the way* to the top. You didn't ask. You *yelled* at me.'

'Just let me have your washing.'

'Let me get *in*—'

'I'm back at work now, remember; I haven't got all day. Which bag's it in, this one?' Mum bent to unzip it which brought Rosie thundering down the stairs.

'Get out of it! That's private! Leave it alone!'

'Then come and unpack it yourself.'

Rosie picked up the bag and lugged it towards the staircase.

'Where are you taking it? Empty it here, it won't take a moment. I only want your dirty clothes.'

'Why, do you want to watch me? You don't trust me, I haven't been home five minutes and—'

'You haven't been home five minutes and already you've started a row.'

Rosie couldn't read the warning signals. There'd never been any before.

'*I've* started a row? *I've* started a row? Get off my case you—'

'*Shut up!*' Mum screamed. Rosie was so startled she dropped the bag and it rolled to the foot of the stairs like a murder victim. 'Shut up, you hateful, *hateful* brat. You've never got a nice word to say for anyone, I'm sick of the sight and sound of you already. Leave that bag – *leave it!* – go upstairs and stay there until I tell you to come down. Go on, get out of my sight.'

Rosie stood there half-way up the stairs, her mouth open. I expect mine was too. No one had ever spoken to her like that – correction – none of *us* had ever spoken to her like that. Where were the jokes? Where was the tolerance? Where was Gran to drawl, *'Aren't you full of the joys of spring, my little organ-pipe cactus?'*

'I meant it, go to your room. I don't want to see you or hear you. No, you can't have a drink. Go away! Get out!' Mum was still shouting, although there wasn't any need to shout now. Rosie's eyes were filling with real tears. She started to come down.

'Mummy . . .'

Mum took a step towards her, almost baring her teeth. Rosie turned and fled up the stairs. She didn't slam her door. We could hear her crying, not the usual performance of tempestuous sobs, but stifled, as if she was trying not to.

'Oh, Christ,' Mum said. She picked up the bags and carried them into the kitchen. 'No, I'll see to it,' she said when I tried to take them.

Rosie had certainly had it coming, I wasn't too bothered about her, in fact I was looking forward to the time when she was allowed down and had to say sorry. It was Mum I was thinking of, but she'd made it clear she didn't want me around just then and I didn't want to risk catching what Rosie had caught. Rosie had always been regarded as a storm that would blow itself out eventually. Was there room in the house for two hurricanes at once?

Rosie was still subdued when Gran came back two days later. I'd never been so glad to see her.

Mum was at work when her taxi drew up and I ran out to meet her. I was in my room but after she'd rung from Heathrow I'd been listening out, with all the doors and windows open, for that unmistakeable ticking-over of a diesel engine. She'd said not to bother Roger about meeting her as the local coach was due at any second and there wasn't time to explain that this was just as well.

'How was the flight?'

'A red-eye. As grisly as usual, with the added excitement of wondering about the political sympathies of your fellow passengers.'

'Coffee?'

'Hot and strong. I'll just go down and say hullo to Roj.'

'He's not there,' I said. 'I mean, he's not here.'

'Where's he gone?'

I had to tell her I didn't know and I saw real alarm in her eyes.

'You mean he's just – gone? Anna didn't say anything.'

'No, nothing like that. He's seeing someone in Preston – it's work – and he thought he'd drive around for a few days on his own, a bit more holiday. You know, the Dales, the Lake District . . .'

'Oh. For one awful moment I thought—'

We looked at each other. Dad had never done anything like that before. He didn't even like being away overnight if he had to go and see clients. I'd known him drive home at three in the morning.

I made the coffee and we sat outside the French windows, going through Gran's photographs in which Beatrice looked more than ever like Walks Tall Wolf Woman. She'd brought presents for all of us – mine was a leather folder with Haida Indian designs worked on it, the sort of thing you see on totem poles. The second week of the visit they'd driven up to Vancouver, which isn't very far – in North American terms. I wanted to go there more than ever.

'Anything interesting happen while I've been away?'

I'd been wondering what to tell her, rows with Jamze, rows with Rosie, Mum being on edge, Dad being caustic, everyone acting unnaturally polite in between. And, at intervals, phone calls that no one talked about. I reckoned she'd find out soon enough.

Thinking about those phone calls I had reasoned that if they had anything to hide Sandor would ring Mum on her mobile, or text her although he'd said he didn't know how and I could believe that. But whatever Sandor did he would want as many people as possible to know about it. At first I'd felt really sorry for him, putting the scent in the washing machine, sitting alone in the dark, and I thought of that John Donne poem, the man writing about a dead woman on the longest night of the year: ' 'Tis the year's midnight, and it is the day's.' But lately I'd been thinking, like Dad, Why do we have to know that? I'd been on the verge of checking her phone for messages, and then I felt really sick. What was Clay Winchester doing, even thinking about snooping in a lady's private personal possessions? Shoot first, ask questions afterwards was one thing, but poking about because you were afraid to ask questions, much less shoot, that was quite different. How could I look Wild Bill Hickok and Bat Masterson in the eye? What would Wyatt Earp say to that low-down rattlesnake?

Probably Wyatt Earp wouldn't take a blind bit of notice. The true facts about the gunfight at the OK Corral suggest that on the moral side there wasn't all that much to choose between the Earps and the

Clantons. History is written by the winners. Would one want the Earps living next door? One asks oneself. The real Wyatt Earp died in his bed in 1929, not quite sixty years before I was born. We shared a century. Wyatt Earp, the scourge of Tombstone, listened to the radio and made telephone calls. In his lifetime the Atlantic was crossed by air.

It was no use. I couldn't see anything funny in what I'd almost done. All I told Gran about were my GCSEs.

When Dad came home we had the first sit-down supper, all six of us, since the beginning of the holidays. It went off quietly, everyone on their best behaviour (including Gran who'd evidently picked up the bad vibes); no grunts from Jamze, no strops from Rosie, not much of anything from anyone else – and no phone calls. It was less best behaviour than wariness. Dad talked about the Lake District and Yorkshire. He'd brought back a Wensleydale cheese. Gran talked about the West Coast.

After supper the Iversons dropped in for a drink on their way home from somewhere and talked openly about the one thing we'd all been avoiding. It was getting late by then, Jamze and Rosie had already disappeared and I was bowing out on account of the paper round. As I passed the door of the front room on my way upstairs I heard Penny saying, 'Well, he seems to be coming to terms with it at last.'

John said something about phone calls and Penny said, 'Well, I suppose he had to tell someone.'

Dad: Some*one*?

John: Don't tell me he's been calling you as well.

Dad: Not me, actually.

Mum: Perhaps he tried us if you were out.

Penny: Or vice versa. It did get a bit exhausting, but he was taking it so badly. When he told me about putting the scent in the washing machine—

Mum: He told *you* about putting the scent in the washing machine?

John: You mean, you got it too?

Dad: The sleepless nights, the lone vigils in the dark?

John: That wasn't as bad as the day she left him.

Penny: Oh, the Great Escape – Gatwick—

John: Dropped in on the way back—

Mum: Ali?

Penny: No, Sandor.

Gran: I seem to have missed the best bit. Shame.

Mum: When was that, the eighteenth? We got him on the nineteenth.

Dad: Talk about freedom of information.

Penny: We shouldn't be laughing.

All: No, no; we shouldn't . . . no . . .

But they did, one after the other and then all together. They practically had hysterics. I stood on the landing and listened. It must have been like that during World War II, hearing the All Clear after an air raid, the release of tension, the relief.

You might not have heard another bomber coming over, Tail-end Charlie.

Seven

Going back to school at the beginning of the autumn term can be quite stressful, but after our summer it was almost relaxing. Rosie started at the Upper School and became strangely quiet. Jamze entered Year Eleven and reality hit – GCSE. I knew it wouldn't last, though, and it was the thought of those two muddying my waters that had made me persuade Mum and Dad to let me do A level at the FE instead of Sixth Form.

It took longer to get there because it would have been suicidal to cycle on the ring road, but I kept up the paper round. It was good for me. Some people do vigorous exercises first thing in the morning. I deliver papers.

I never saw any signs of life from 107 Addington Road and things seemed to be getting back to normal when, one Sunday morning, the phone rang.

As I picked up the handset in the hall I wasn't

expecting to hear Sandor's voice – that's how relaxed we'd got – or I had, at any rate.

Sandor said, 'That sounds like Clay.'

I grunted, just like Jamze.

'Is Anna there?'

'She's cooking the lunch.'

'Oh, what time do you eat?'

You've got a nerve, I thought, getting the impression that he was going to invite himself round for a meal. 'One thirty, today.'

'Do you think it would be all right if I dropped round for a few minutes – I just need a quick word.'

I wondered how he'd react if I said no, it wouldn't be all right.

'I'll ask her,' I said, 'or I could get her to ring you later.'

He didn't seem to like that idea. 'I'm at a friend's house,' he said. 'Hang on, I'll just find out when they're eating . . .'

I heard him put the receiver down on what sounded like a table, and then a door opening, and then silence.

'Hullo?' I said. 'Hullo?' Stupid. You can always tell when there's no one there. The silence went on and on. Then a man's voice said loudly, not to me, 'Well, I don't know what we're supposed to do about it.'

214

A woman answered, I couldn't hear what she said but it was the sound of someone trying to be reasonable.

Then the man said, 'I don't see why we have to be involved.'

The woman again; pleading? Pacifying?

Then the man: 'He's your friend, not mine. I hardly know him.'

Where had I heard that before? It was obvious that Sandor had forgotten that he'd left the phone off the hook and had gone away, and some kind of row had broken out the moment the door closed behind him.

It wasn't John and Penny . . . was it?

The man – no, it wasn't John – shouted, 'Do what you like! Leave me out of it! I want nothing to do with it! If I hear any more about scent in the washing machine—'

I put the phone down.

Just as obvious was the fact that whoever they were they had no idea that anyone was listening to them. I waited a few minutes and then pressed 1471 in the hope that they'd seen the phone and hung up. They had, and an 0208 number was quoted; Outer London. If Sandor was going to call in for a few minutes it wouldn't be before lunch, that was clear, even if he drove like the clappers. Perhaps he would time his entrance for the middle of the meal. Perhaps he would crash the car.

But who were they, this couple who had erupted into a furious argument the moment Sandor had left them? How many more people did he know who were falling out because of him and Ali? There must be households all over southern England getting caught up in this dispute that had nothing to do with them, like Belgium being invaded after Gavrilo Prinzip shot Archduke Franz Ferdinand at Sarajevo in 1914. What did that have to do with Belgium? Nothing, they just happened to be in the way and wouldn't, couldn't, get out of it. Result? World War I.

I went into the kitchen.

'Sandor,' I said, 'on the phone.'

'What did he want?' Mum was making salad dressing. She seemed to be paying more attention to the vinaigrette than to the prospect of Sandor turning up, but what did I know?

'He's going to drop in for a few minutes, he said.'

'When?'

'He called from London. It won't be for an hour at least.'

She didn't ask how I knew or who he'd been with. Perhaps she knew, perhaps she didn't.

Mum and Dad have always been very firm about Sunday lunch. The rest of the week we could do as we pleased about meals so long as we gave advance warning, but apart from Gran who was sometimes working late, most of us showed up most of the time, and Rosie was not yet given an option, cue more strops. But Sundays, at one thirty, we all ate together, six of us, that number that the dining table could seat comfortably. It was usually a roast in winter and salads in summer, very traditional. Rosie had been a vegetarian for a time.

'Fine,' Mum had said. 'If you're serious about it I'll cook you separate dishes, but if you lapse, just *once*, you can go back to being a meat-eater like the rest of us.' Personally I thought that Rosie was being a vegetarian simply to make life difficult for Mum and in the hope that the rest of us would feel uneasy eating our fellow creatures while she grazed on leaves, but Mum and Dad had always liked us to have personal ethics and you couldn't argue with anyone being a vegetarian on ethical grounds. For a fortnight Rosie was a vegan – which did make life extremely difficult and if you've ever necked a mouthful of soya milk by mistake you will know what I mean, but she didn't give up wearing leather shoes – and an ordinary common or garden vegetarian for about a month after that. Then Gran saw her coming out of KFC with some mates and a large greasy-looking bucket.

That was the end of it, although Rosie predictably created.

Rosie: You can't expect me to give up all at once!

Gran: Certainly we can. It's not like giving up cigarettes or booze. You're not addicted to meat, are you? You won't have to go on a twelve-step programme to kick the habit, standing up to say, 'My name is Rose and I am a carnivore,' at Flesh-eaters Anonymous. Are we going to find cans of corned beef hidden in the wardrobe?

Rosie: It's not funny! You want me to lose all my friends because I'm a vegetarian!

Gran: No we don't. If they're your friends they'll respect your principles. You might even convert them, then you can all live on roots and berries.

We had a nice lunch and washed up and dispersed

as usual. Rosie had forgotten that she was at the mercy of marauding paedophiles and there was the usual row about where she was going and who she was going to be with – 'I can't stand this, you expect me to tell you every move I make, I can't do *anything* without everyone knowing about it, haven't you heard of *privacy*?' – Gran went out, Dad said he'd cut the grass. Jamze had already vanished in that serpentine way he has when there is a chance he may be asked to assist with something.

By now it was three o'clock.

'What time did Sandor say he'd be round?' Mum said.

'He didn't.'

'I thought you said about an hour.'

'I was guessing. He rang from London. I just assumed it would be at least an hour.'

'Whereabouts in London? If he's south of the river—'

'He didn't say.' And I didn't say how I'd discovered where he was, nor what he'd said about finding out when his hosts were having lunch, because he'd obviously left the house soon after he put the phone down.

'It shouldn't be too long,' Mum said. 'I'll wait in. He didn't say what it was about?'

As if one couldn't guess.

'It didn't sound very urgent,' I said. 'You can see him at work tomorrow, can't you? He can always ring again. You go out if you want, I'll be here.'

'No . . . I'm going to put my feet up with the papers and listen to the lawnmower. The sweetest sound, other people busting a gut. What are you doing?'

'Coursework,' I said, 'then I might go over to Daisy's.'

By five o'clock Sandor still hadn't shown up. When I went down Mum was doing the crossword, the really tough one without any black squares, and hadn't noticed the time.

'Tea, coffee, light refreshments?' I said, looking in at the door.

'Is that the time?' People always say that, looking at a clock, as though the clock should have said something sooner. 'I hope nothing's happened.'

'What? Oh, Sandor. It's a nice day, weekend traffic . . .'

'He might have rung. He'll have his mobile.'

Yes, I thought, he'll have his mobile. So why use a land line and leave the phone off the hook? Even *those* friends had to be involved.

'I'll just give him a call.'

I made tea. When I got back she was looking puzzled. 'No one's answering at home and the mobile's switched off,' she said. 'I left a message on both. You don't think he's had an accident?'

I had a shot of the Audi, a crumpled wreck in a ditch off the motorway with the mobile ringing pathetically, like a dog that doesn't know Master has died and is waiting for him to come home.

She rang several times during the evening with the same result: 277272, I knew those beeps by heart.

'I expect he's gone off somewhere,' I said, 'and forgotten about it.'

'Probably . . . can't help worrying, though.'

Why worry about *him*? I thought. Do you think he worries about us? And I kept telling myself, if there was anything going on, she wouldn't let me know about it. After that evening when the Iversons came round I'd not been worrying so much myself and I didn't want to start again.

But I noticed that she didn't say anything to Dad although that could have been because he had made it clear that he was so very not interested in Sandor Harker. In the end I didn't go over to Daisy because I wanted to keep an eye on things at my end.

So that was another day buggered up, for at least one of us.

Coming down Addington Road next morning I noticed, while forcing the *Independent* through the minute letter box at 84, that the Audi was parked outside 107.

As a sign, I thought cynically. Ali's gone, the garage is vacant, but he leaves it outside. Surely he can't be sleeping in it this time. As I got closer I saw that no, the car was not occupied but the house seemed to be. Although the sun was up I could see a light through the glass panel in the front door. Then I noticed that the light was on in the living room, the one that had a window on to the porch, and in the other front room too. And the glass door that opened on to the balcony upstairs was lit up. Had something happened, had he really had an accident? Not on the motorway but indoors, falling downstairs? Should I care?

I didn't, and I didn't really believe anything had happened but . . . there was his failure to appear yesterday, the unanswered phone calls and messages. How would it feel if it turned out that he was lying injured and helpless at the foot of the stairs – or worse. I imagined Mum saying, 'But you saw the lights on and you did nothing?' Why should I do anything? Supposing he was dead or injured and I kept what I had seen to myself; it would gnaw at me, I should always feel guilty.

I parked the bike by the fence and went up into the porch where I peered through the window into the L-shaped living room.

It looked exactly as it had done the last time I saw it. I'd had some mental image of Sandor distracted (well, that's the word he'd used), neglecting the housekeeping, living off takeaways and descending into squalor, but everything was perfectly tidy, newspapers neatly squared off on the coffee table, cushions plumped up in the corners of the sofa, the pot plants flourishing and well-watered. House plants are always the first to suffer when people go downhill. The only thing wrong was the lamp, all the lamps, burning by daylight.

I rang the bell and knocked. There was no answer, no sound from inside. I tried looking through the letter flap but they had one of those draught-excluder brushes on the other side. The front room window was higher up because the garden sloped, but when I stepped off the porch and went round to it I found I was tall enough to see in; polished table, chairs lined up on both sides of it, empty fruit bowl in the middle. And the light on.

Were the neighbours watching me? I half hoped someone was, the *Rear Window* lady perhaps, someone who would come and ask me what I was up to, give the perfectly simple explanation that I wanted to hear, offer to do something. People who are going to be away often leave lights burning, to deter burglars, but they don't leave the curtains open so that the burglars can see the place is empty.

As I was now at the corner of the house I carried on across the gravel in front of the garage and round the side to the area I'd seen during the party, with the compost bin and wheelbarrow. That took me past the side window of the kitchen, all lit up like the others.

The kitchen was not so tidy. Unlike my last sight of it when I had thought it looked like a set piece from a catalogue, it actually showed some signs of use. That is, it didn't look as if anyone had been cooking in there but there were lots of bottles standing about, empty ones on the draining board.

I moved on – here came the ornamental bamboo again – and knocked at the back door, loudly, remembering how Rosie and I had cowered upstairs while Gran went from front door to back, hammering to be let in and, just like Gran, I took out my phone and called Sandor's number that I knew so well, 277272. I heard the ringing inside but it did what ours does; rang seven times until the electronic woman intercepted it.

I knocked again, I was about to try the handle, and then I heard *someone else* knocking, at the front door. I could hear it in stereo, the sound from outside travelling round the house and from inside travelling through it.

Postman? I hadn't seen a postman and it was a bit early for post in Addington Road on a Monday. Milkman pursuing an unpaid bill? No, there were already full bottles on the step. But a grown-up, I thought pathetically, even if it's only *Rear Window* lady. I went back the way I'd come, hoping to catch whoever it was, but the porch was empty. Then I saw that the tall side gate in the hedge was open. I was about to make a dive for it when I had a preview of whoever-it-was following my route around the house so that we ended up chasing each other, which is no doubt very funny to watch but not when it's you doing it. Instead I doubled back fast, past the garage, and it worked. As I passed the kitchen I heard knocking on the back door and when I came round the corner there was a man just walking away, looking up at the first-floor windows as he went.

I called out, 'Wait!' louder than I meant to because he was only a few metres away, and he whipped round as if he expected a mugger to leap out of the bamboo. I thought it was Sandor.

It was Oz.

He recognized me, I could tell, but he didn't remember who I was at first, or where he'd met me.

'Hi, Oz,' I said. 'It's Clay. I was at that party.'

I didn't need to remind him which party.

'Of course,' he said. 'What are you doing here? Not looking for Dad?' He didn't say, 'At this hour?' Perhaps he was used to strange women trying to break in to get at his father, but I could see he was puzzled.

'I'm on my paper round,' I said. 'Sandor was supposed to be coming round to ours yesterday but he didn't turn up and he wasn't answering the phone – any phone. And then I was cycling past and I saw all the lights on.'

Oz's puzzled look turned to one of alarm.

'I was supposed to be having dinner with him last night but, same here, no show. Then some friends he'd been staying with rang me—'

'From London?'

'Yes, as it happens. They were worried. He'd been drinking but he drove off in such a hurry he'd left their phone off the hook.'

'That was us he was ringing,' I said. 'I took the call. Do you think he's had an accident?'

'No pile-ups on the M40 yesterday,' Oz said. 'I checked.'

'Perhaps he wasn't on the M40.'

'Dad take a back road?' Oz said sourly. 'Never. He might pass unnoticed.'

Oh Oz, lovely Oz. Of all the grown-ups I'd hoped for, the right one had shown up.

'Anyway, the car's out at the front,' I said. 'I meant an accident indoors. Have you got a key?'

'Yes, for the front door, but it's bolted from the inside. I bet this one is too.'

I suddenly wasn't so sure and turned the door knob. It opened. I said, and I was taking a risk, 'It would be a pity if no one could get in, wouldn't it?' because I was thinking to myself that Sandor knew perfectly well that even if no one else tried to find him, I'd be the one to see the lights on.

Oz gave me a very funny look which said, 'Got it in one' and we went in. The kitchen smelled of booze, from all those unwashed empties, and a dark sticky patch on the floor which I thought for a minute must be blood. We looked in the L-shaped bit of the living room that wasn't visible from the porch and in the dining room which was empty, as I'd seen through the window.

Oz reached out to switch off the light and then drew his hand back. 'Don't touch anything,' he said, and I realized, from all those television crime scenes, that he was really worried and thinking ahead to the police arriving. He started towards the stairs and I almost expected him to say, 'You'd better stay here,' which is what men are gallantly meant to say, but he didn't. I felt he was glad he had someone with him and it was only then that I had to admit what we were both afraid of finding: a suicide.

We looked in all the upstairs rooms; curtains open, lights on, nobody home.

'Where *is* he?' Oz said, and forgetting about not touching anything, sat down heavily on the bed in Sandor's room. It hadn't been made, in fact it looked like Tracey Emin's bed, but there was no sign of a struggle. 'What do we do now? Start checking the cupboards?' He lifted the valance and looked underneath. 'What have we missed?'

I remembered my reconnaissance during the

party. 'Downstairs loo.' Down we went again. The door of the little cloakroom was shut and when Oz pushed it it wouldn't open although it gave slightly. It wasn't locked. He turned to me and he had gone very pale.

'There's something behind it,' he said. 'Someone.'

Oz is a big bloke and I am not small but it took our combined weight to shift whatever was behind the door far enough for Oz to squeeze through. I stayed outside and put my head round it. Sandor was collapsed on the floor between the wash-hand basin at one end and the lavatory at the other, half sitting against the door, feet against the opposite wall. Our shoving had kind of concertinaed him. I couldn't see his face, his head was hanging down. He didn't seem to be breathing.

'Is he dead?' I could only whisper it.

Oz crouched down by his father and lifted his head slightly. Sandor let out a frightful snort, like a startled horse, and his head lolled again. The small room filled with fumes.

'Dead drunk,' Oz said. 'Must have passed out in here – I don't suppose that was part of the plot.'

'What are we going to do?'

'I've a good mind to leave him here,' Oz muttered

furiously. 'I wouldn't want to have his head when he wakes up.'

'He ought to be in the recovery position.'

Oz remarked that he ought to be somewhere else that I didn't quite catch.

'I suppose we should move him,' he said aloud. 'Can we manage something between us? Do you mind?'

It took quite a bit of manoeuvring – with the two of us and the body in that confined space – to shift Sandor far enough to get the door opened back against the wall; then with a couple of three-point turns, me at the feet, Oz at the heavy end, we got him out into the hall.

'Upstairs?'

'I have my lower back to consider,' Oz said. 'So have you. Sofa. Living room.'

It was a very large sofa. We unloaded him on to it and turned him over, three-quarters prone, as they tell you in first aid instructions. Sandor was by now snoring in fitful gusts.

Oz stood looking down at him wearily.

'Coffee?' I said.

'Many litres – hey, look, this was great of you, but won't you be expected somewhere?'

'Ohmygod!' It was a quarter to eight. Kindly,

worried Mr Mirza would be wondering where I'd got to. They might even have noticed at home. I zipped into the kitchen, switched on the kettle and made a couple of calls. I told Mr M that a friend had had an accident but that I was quite safe and would drop off the bag later; then I rang home.

It was Dad who answered, the last person I wanted to tell; the last person who wanted to know. I could hear him controlling his temper at the other end.

'Why, exactly, did you feel you had to go looking for this drama queen?'

'Well, he was supposed to be coming round yesterday and—' and there were all those calls Mum had made that possibly Dad didn't know about. 'I saw all the lights on, and then I ran into Oz.'

'*Who* is Oz?'

'His son – remember? At the party.'

'Ah, yes, the family adult,' Dad said. 'Are you coming home now?'

'We're just going to have coffee and then I'll be back. Can you tell Mum—'

I was just about to wish I hadn't said that when he said, 'No, I don't think so. You've got everything under control, haven't you; between you?'

'Yes.'

'Then I don't think Anna needs to know. I'll give you a cover story.'

He thought she'd come rushing round to 107 too, I suppose, not in the throes of passion, just concerned, as everybody had to be concerned.

'I'll see you later, then. Watch out for the Canadians.' It was ages since he'd said that.

Oz had come into the kitchen while I was talking and was washing his hands very thoroughly at the sink. 'I think we might treat ourselves to breakfast,' he said, 'on the house.' He opened the fridge. It looked very well stocked for someone teetering on the edge of despair.

'Eggs, bacon, tomatoes, steak . . .' Oz offered.

'Toast?'

We made toast and coffee and breakfasted standing up at the window looking out over the garden, the way Dad does. Every few minutes a shattering rasp came from the living room. The fourth time, Oz closed the door.

'Suppose he chokes?'

'He's in the recovery position, isn't he? Anyway, I can still hear him. Look, forgive my asking, but how do you come to be involved in this?'

'I don't know,' I said. 'We're all involved – except

Jamze and Rosie. You haven't met them – my brother and sister.'

'Well, hooray for them,' Oz said. 'The man's like a black hole – everything gets sucked in.'

Including Rosie and Jamze, now that I thought about it. 'Ali got out.'

'After accusing just about every woman we know of having an affair with him.'

'Where is she now?'

'Back home in Rotherham firing off solicitor's letters. Clay, I'm not trying to get rid of you or anything but—'

'I know, I have to get to school.' I started to rinse out the coffee mug and then changed my mind and refilled it. 'No I don't. I'm at the FE now. I haven't got a class till ten.' I hadn't got used to that yet.

'I just don't like to think of you embroiled in this mess.'

I never have responded to protectiveness.

'I want to know, if you don't mind . . . *why*? I know he's your dad and all that, but apart from that, he's no one special, is he?'

'In what way special?' Oz said, smiling slightly and getting himself another coffee. It was instant but of a very superior kind, not the sort Mr Mirza stocks at the convenience counter next to the chiller cabinet.

'Well, it's all a bit "Curse of *Hello!*" isn't it? You know, the garden party, with everybody watching . . .'

'Exclusive pictures of Mr and Mrs Alexander Harker in their lovely home.'

'And then it all goes pear-shaped. I mean, it was going pear-shaped that afternoon, wasn't it?'

'You're very observant,' Oz said. 'And there we were, thinking we were keeping up appearances. That wasn't the beginning of it by a long chalk, but things had come to a head, as they do with monotonous regularity where Dad is concerned. Why they had to throw a party when they were barely speaking to each other—'

'Like they almost wanted to have people watch?'

Oz sat on the table, swinging his feet. 'I ought to be getting to work,' he said fretfully, half to himself. 'Oh, sod it, they can start without me.'

'Who?'

'It's just a meeting, they can get the housekeeping out of the way first. I'll give them a call in a minute.'

'You're standing for parliament, aren't you?' I said.

'Did he tell you that? No, I was selected by the Eastbridge Ward of the Lib Dems to stand for the city council in May – the Greens wiped the floor with us. But that wasn't glamorous enough for his stage set.'

'Stage set?'

'It's all stage design, scene setting, hadn't you noticed?' Oz said. I thought of something Dad had said about audience participation and the back row of the one and nines. 'This all goes back to his last divorce.'

'How many's he had, then?'

'Oh, just the one, so far, and now this. I meant my parents splitting up.'

'Why did they?' I said.

He thought about it. 'You might say Mum didn't mind being the straight half of a double act, she didn't mind being the stooge, she didn't mind being the feed, she just resented being part of the scenery. Ali, I assume, has come to the same conclusion.'

'She's not dead, then?'

'Mum? No – whoever said she was? Not *Dad*?'

'Oh no.' I blushed. It had just come to me what I had said, and why I had said it.

Oz laughed. 'What's the matter? Were you suspecting foul play? I don't think that's part of the image.'

I had to tell him about *Rear Window* and our theory, Dad's and mine, that the first Mrs Harker was under the rose bushes. He laughed even harder and I laughed too and we were both saying, 'It's not *funny*,' which made it much more difficult to stop.

'Actually,' Oz said, 'we're lucky, you and I. We're only sitting in the back row. It really isn't funny for the Iversons and the Machins, and your parents.'

'Who are the Machins?'

'He was with them yesterday, when he rang you.'

'They had a mammoth row after he'd gone,' I said. 'I heard it start – then I hung up,' I added, before he could ask.

'Mammoth rows break out wherever he goes,' Oz said. 'Wake turbulence.'

'What, like behind boats?'

'I was thinking more of planes,' Oz said. 'If a smaller aircraft takes off too close behind a 747 it can get caught in the wake turbulence. It happened over a New York suburb a few years ago. The second plane fell out of the sky, killed everyone on board and more on the ground. The 747 flew on, innocent and unaware. Dad flies on, unaware, and everything crashes behind him.'

'He knows what he's doing though, doesn't he? You can't call him innocent.' I had a picture of a jumbo jet, a machine the size of a factory, wings spread, oddly serene, utterly self-contained, disinterested, and quite unable to look over its shoulder to see the turmoil behind it, and I knew what Oz meant.

'Not innocent in the sense of blameless, harmless,' he said, 'but certainly without any idea of cause and effect. He's an attention-seeker, nothing can simply happen to him, it has to be dramatized, bells and whistles . . .'

'Like Rosie.' How had we failed to notice what was going on with Rosie under our noses?

'How old is Rosie?'

'Eleven.'

'Fair enough in an eleven-year-old. What we have here is a forty-eight-year-old. It wasn't enough that lovely little Ali falls in love and marries him – she's my age, my stepmother. Had you thought of that? He couldn't just tell himself how lucky he was, he had to let her know how tremendously lucky *she* was, you know: "Women find me irresistible, but I chose you." '

'Do they find him irresistible?'

'Well, you don't, obviously,' Oz said, 'but he's ace at being the centre of attention, isn't he? Everyone is tremendously *concerned* about him – Julia Machin, Penny Iverson, to name but two, while on the sidelines stand bemused husbands wondering what's hit them.'

'And Gran, and Mum,' I said. 'Even me, a bit.'

'Is your father bemused?'

'The first time Sandor came to our house Dad said to me, "Who the hell is he?" He wasn't very pleased just now when I rang.'

'How much did you tell him?'

'Not a lot,' I said, 'just that you and I had found Sandor – he was all right about it when I said you were here.'

'Good of him. He's only met me once.'

'He called you the family adult.'

'I'm not the only one,' he said. 'You haven't met my mother or sisters.'

'Sisters?'

'Lucasta and Cressida; we were part of the scenery too; fancy names, classy schools he couldn't really afford, shunted towards glittering careers we didn't want. Luke's a plumber, Cress has a degree in engineering and I'm in the probation service. We had to go in the end. We were not worthy.'

'Why do you go on seeing him?' I said. It really was time for Oz to go to work and me to go to FE but in spite of all the upheaval that had gone on I was feeling rather happy, leaning against the sink drinking coffee in what was a very nice kitchen, talking to Oz, a very nice man.

'Someone has to keep an eye on the silly sod,' Oz

said, 'and he *is* my father. These flocks of worried women are all very well but if one of them did respond with cries of "Take me, you horny beast, I'm yours," you wouldn't see him for dust. He thinks he likes women, but he doesn't. They just make good decor. If he got caught with someone even approximately his own age he'd be afraid of looking old. Your father has nothing to fear. Histrionics aside, losing Ali has upset him, of course it has, but not quite as much as he'd like everyone to think. There'll be another along, presently.'

He saw me out through the front door. The noise of the bolts being drawn provoked sounds of life from the living room. 'Seems like I might be able to get to work quite soon,' Oz said. He started to open the door and then said suddenly, 'Clay, you're a hero. Let me give you a hug.'

He did, and a kiss, not sexy, just friendly. Sandor would have opened the door first and done it on the step in case someone might be watching, so that he could spring back guiltily. Oz stood in the porch and waved as I mounted the bike and rode away.

I didn't fill Dad in on the details of that last Sunday, or of my conversation with Oz in the kitchen. I would have done, if he'd asked, but he didn't. He already knew more than he wanted to. I told Gran and Mum, though, both at the same time so that there would be no doubt at all about who knew what.

Mum was upset at my graphic description of our adventures in the downstairs loo, not about Sandor but at the thought of me being exposed to such scenes of squalor at my tender age. I began to wonder if she'd looked at me lately.

'Don't be daft,' Gran said. 'You've had me in the house for years. Who's been corrupted?'

'We all have,' I said.

Mum snapped, 'It's not funny!'

Where had I heard that before? We both rounded on her. 'Yes it is!'

But Mum still didn't laugh. I suppose she was thinking about how close we had all come to crashing in flames. 'Roger should have told me what was going on as soon as you called. He just said you'd met a friend and would be going straight on to college.'

'I was with a friend. I was with Oz.'

'I'd have come straight over—'

'That's exactly why Roj didn't tell you,' Gran said. 'If you'd turned up overflowing with sympathy we'd still have him hanging around our necks like a bleeding albatross. I told you he was one of the undead. You and Oz should have put him out in the sun, Clay, and he'd have turned to dust.'

'She should never have been involved,' Mum said. 'None of us should.'

My sentiments entirely, I thought.

All I said to Dad was, 'The first Mrs Harker isn't buried in the flower bed. She lives in Ealing with a man who designs firework displays.'

Dad just said, 'That must be quite restful after life with The Man Who Came To Dinner.'

I'd taken some milk down to the studio to replace the latest batch of cottage cheese which was festering on the window sill.

Dad put it down to global warming. 'When I were a lad we could make a bottle of milk last a week without a fridge.'

'All fifteen of you?'

'I may have miscounted. It might only have been twelve but they would keep moving about.' (Dad is in fact the younger of two, although his sister, my Aunt Susan, went to Australia and had seven children.)

I took the carton outside and emptied the cottage cheese over the compost heap before it set solid and became Parmesan. When I came back Dad was examining the video library.

'Fancy an evening at the movies?'

'Before we eat or after?'

'We could fit in a short before dinner. Buster Keaton? Gene Autry, Oklahoma's Yodelling Cowboy and his horse Champion . . . ?'

'After dinner we'd have time for *Nosferatu*.'

'What made you think of that?'

'Something Gran said . . .' *Nosferatu* is the first attempt to film *Dracula*, and the vampire is not one of your suave types in evening dress, with slicked-back hair and fangs. He has ratty front teeth and fly-away ears, and when the rising sun strikes him he doesn't turn to dust, just dissolves in its healing rays.

'Do you think she'd like to watch?'

'Eh?'

'Marina; she's the vampire buff.'

'I think she's going out. No, just us.'

Nosferatu is on the same tape as *Mary Poppins* which Rosie used to adore before her horns came through. Dad put the cassette in the machine and pressed fast forward.

He said, awkwardly, 'You know, you don't have to.'

'Don't have to what?'

'Come down here and watch ancient movies with your ancient father. You must have better things to do.'

'Homework? We don't call it that any more, we FE types, doncherknow? Anyway, there's nothing urgent. I got a lot done in the college library before I came home.'

'I wasn't thinking of your homework. Isn't there anything you'd rather . . . anyone else you'd rather be with?'

'No.'

'Well, far be it from me to encourage you to neglect your studies for a life of debauchery,' he said, and didn't even finish because the counter had come up to 140. Poppins had popped off.

'Debauchery? Watching videos with you?'

'It was the alternatives I was thinking of. Look, Clay, sooner or later you *are* going to want to say, "Thanks Dad but no thanks." When the time comes, for God's sake say it, don't come and watch with me because you haven't the heart to refuse. What do you think I'll do, dig myself into the compost heap and mope?'

'No—'

'Because I won't. Don't *ever* do anything because you're sorry for me. You're only marking time at the moment but when the band strikes up and you're ready to go, *go*.'

Sorry for him? Sorry for my dad? For a moment I had to think about it. I wasn't, never had been; but it had been a near thing.

And was I marking time? I liked that. Maybe I wasn't a late developer or a man-hater, just fussy. When I spotted a bloke who was worth the effort I'd make the effort, now that I had a standard to measure him by.

Up to that point I'd only had Dad and I'd never been able to imagine him as anything *but* Dad. I'd never given much thought to his back story in spite of seeing pictures of him when he was a young man; Roger Winchester the plate-layer's son, printer's apprentice; I bet I'd have liked him, though.

I wasn't getting any ideas about Oz. I was just pleased that he liked me and I hoped I'd see him again. And he'd given me a standard to measure myself by. I was a hero. I'd been told that by someone who knew what he was talking about. In future I wouldn't look at anyone who didn't think so too.

Oz must have been stern with his father when he was in a condition to pay attention. Oz, of course, the family adult, had long ago given up thinking of Sandor as just 'Dad'. And I wondered how Sandor thought of Oz who looked so like him but wasn't like him at all in any other way. You could safely take off behind Oz without crashing.

And every morning I went on cycling down Addington Road, past 107 at the corner. I still looked at it, it was impossible not to, and I wondered what was going on inside because, although Sandor still worked at DDI and I suppose Mum still ran into him sometimes, he had faded from our lives. We didn't even get a Christmas card. I hope we didn't send one. In a way Oz and I had done just what Gran had said, put him out in the sun; and when you could see him properly, he wasn't there.

But one spring morning, an unexpectedly warm day in March, while I was jamming the *Indy* through the flap at 84, I looked up and saw the curtain moving at the door on to the balcony above the porch at 107. As I rode towards it the door opened and a woman came out, in a dressing gown, a woman or a girl, she didn't look much older than me. There were daffodils and polyanthus in the flower tubs, the sun was up, just enough to highlight her and the flowers. She stood there smiling. I couldn't help waving up at her as I went past, and she leaned against the railing and waved back, Juliet on the balcony.

I suppose it had just started and already I could see how it would end, but this time I'd take care not to be even in the back row. Black and white is all very well, but it can be misleading. You expect the guys in black hats to be bad, not silly. I stopped to deliver the *Times Educational Supplement* to 193, then hit the trail again, drifting westward over the high plains, me and the tumbling tumbleweeds.